"I've been called 'Princess' enough to last one lifetime, and I know that probably sounds ungrateful when it's many a young girls' dream, but..."

"Let me guess—the reality isn't all it's cracked up to be?"

"No."

He captured her gaze in his. The warmth, the understanding in his crystal clear blues choked up her chest and had the words spilling forth before she could stop them. "Would you understand if I told you my life has been mapped out for years? My parents had a strategy, and I was their pawn to be played to their best advantage."

She bit her lip. Shocked at what she'd admitted. How could she trust him not to spill all? To sell her story like so many others had before? "I shouldn't have—"

She clamped her teeth down so hard she thought she might draw blood, because the truth was, she wanted to talk to him. The urge was like an ever-swelling tide within her. She couldn't explain it. She'd had no one for so long.

"It's okay, Cassie. You can trust me."

Dear Reader,

Sleepwalking is a scary thing, right?

For those dreaming and those observing!

Imagine my surprise when I encountered the behavior for the very first time with my husband. Just like Cassie and Hugo, we weren't married then, either... Though I will admit, we were a little more acquainted.

Years later when it happened again, inspiration struck and the idea for a book was born. Cue me now, writing this letter to you!

Cassie and Hugo took me on such a fabulous adventure around Paris, filling my head and heart with all the imagery and romance of the city, and I hope they fill yours with it all, too!

Beaucoup d'amour et profite bien de Paris <3

Rachael x

FAKE FLING WITH THE BILLIONAIRE

RACHAEL STEWART

ROMANCE

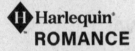

Harlequin®
ROMANCE

ISBN-13: 978-1-335-21610-6

Fake Fling with the Billionaire

Recycling programs for this product may not exist in your area.

Harlequin Enterprises ULC
22 Adelaide St. West, 41st Floor
Toronto, Ontario M5H 4E3, Canada
www.Harlequin.com

Printed in U.S.A.

Rachael Stewart adores conjuring up stories, from heartwarmingly romantic to wildly erotic. She's been writing since she could put pen to paper—as the stacks of scrawled-on pages in her loft will attest to. A Welsh lass at heart, she now lives in Yorkshire, with her very own hero and three awesome kids—and if she's not tapping out a story, she's wrapped up in one or enjoying the great outdoors. Reach her on Facebook, on X (@rach_b52) or at rachaelstewartauthor.com.

Books by Rachael Stewart

Harlequin Romance

Billionaires for the Rose Sisters

Billionaire's Island Temptation
Consequence of Their Forbidden Night

Claiming the Ferrington Empire

Secrets Behind the Billionaire's Return
The Billionaire Behind the Headlines

How to Win a Monroe

Off-Limits Fling with the Heiress
My Unexpected Christmas Wedding

One Year to Wed

Reluctant Bride's Baby Bombshell

My Year with the Billionaire
Unexpected Family for the Rebel Tycoon

Visit the Author Profile page at Harlequin.com.

To all the Dreamers and those that go the
extra-special mile with the sleepwalking,
like those closest to my heart, my hubby,
this one is for you.

xxx

**Praise for
Rachael Stewart**

CHAPTER ONE

Paris. The Witching Hour.

Cassie's favourite time to venture out in recent years. Though she was no witch. No matter how much her ex and his family would like to paint her as such.

She sipped her vodka martini, finding peace in those precious minutes between two and three in the morning while most around her slept.

In the distance, the Eiffel Tower had emitted its final sparkle long enough ago to see the last of the tourists in bed. Its structure a dark silhouette in the inky sky. The avenue of the Champs-Élysées and impressive Arc de Triomphe below flaunted their own muted glow. Equally beautiful in their subtlety, just as reassuring in their solitude too.

'Would you like another, Your Highness?'

Her fingers tightened around the crystal stem of her glass. 'Just Cassie, please, Beni.'

The young waiter bowed his head, his dipped gaze polite. Every night for the past month Beni had opened the rooftop bar for her after hours and every night he had addressed her like so.

Tomorrow, she would still be a princess. And the day after. And the day after that... well, who knew.

Public opinion was a fickle thing, especially when it was fed by the lions—her ex, the Prince of Sérignone. His royal family, the Duponts. Their loyal staff. The world's press.

They'd all crowned her long before her marriage to the Prince...would they go on crowning her long after she was done?

It had been a month. A month divorced. Two years separated. Four years married. Five by his side. A sixth of her life. A sixth she would sooner forget...if only the world would let her.

There was only so long one could bear the title that reminded her of the fool that she had been. The fool that she had let him take her for. And if she was honest, the fool that she had been long before then, courtesy of her parents and their skilled puppeteering from birth.

But she was done dancing to the tunes of

others…it was time to choose her own tune. Her own path. And she couldn't afford for it to be derailed by the vitriol now coming out of Sérignone.

She picked at some invisible lint on her black shift dress as she mentally picked at the remnants of her life. At thirty-three, she'd gone from cherished British socialite to prized princess of a tiny Mediterranean kingdom a thousand kilometres south of where she sat now, as a woman trying to find herself while the world at large tried to keep her pigeon-holed.

Though pigeonholed as a beloved princess beat being painted as the scandalous woman the Duponts and their team of spin doctors were trying to turn her into. Spinning the tale of the woman who had *driven* her husband into the arms of his many lovers. By being emotionally unavailable and 'overfamiliar' with the household staff. Fuelling rumours that she had taken more than one to her bed, because there could be no smoke without fire…not when it worked in their favour. As it did now. Because, in the Duponts' minds, the Prince could not come out of their divorce smelling of roses while she still did.

One of them had to suffer. And so, it had

to be her. Someone had to be blamed for the shocking behaviour of the Prince, and it made most sense—most royal and socioeconomic sense—for that someone to be her.

Didn't matter that she had already suffered enough. *Witnessed* enough. That the behaviour they laid at her door, belonged solely at the Prince's own.

She didn't know what was more galling—to learn that Georges had married her purely for the money, what with the royal reserves in dire need of a cash injection that her father had been all too willing to provide.

Or that she had been naive enough to have believed that she was enough for Georges. That her appeal—her beauty and intelligence, her charity endeavours and European connections, her ability to converse in several languages and win over the people—had been all Georges could have wanted in a princess. That he had wanted her. That he had, as he had told her and she had so desperately wanted to believe, loved her.

But no, it had been a lie and she had been a joke. A laughingstock to all who were in the know. The *real* know.

Behind closed doors. The palace doors. They'd been laughing at her.

Had her parents been cruel enough to laugh too?

They certainly hadn't been laughing when she'd turned up on their doorstep almost two years ago. Desperate for a place to stay. A place to escape to. A place to feel safe from the speculation and the censure and the pain.

They'd only delivered more of the same and tried to force her to return, because heaven forbid, she'd walk out on the Prince and bring shame to their door…

A frenzied stream of reporters too.

'Your Highness?'

She blinked through the painful haze to find Beni still stood over her, waiting expectantly.

'Apologies, Beni. *Ça va, merci.*'

'You are sure?'

No, she wasn't sure. She wouldn't be sure of much for a long time—how she felt, who she could trust, what was real, what was fake, but as far as her need for a drink went, she was done for the night.

'I think I'll head on down, Beni.' She smothered a yawn—at last, sleep beckoned—and rose from her cushioned haven, the scent of the night lifting with her. Far from natural, the fragrance drifted from the inside out…

the hotel's signature scent. Bold and woody, a touch of citrus too. Expensive but heavenly.

She gave him a smile filled with her gratitude. 'Thank you again for this evening.'

'So long as you need the rooftop—' he gave a nod of respect, his brown eyes soft '—it will be here for you.'

If only her own parents had been so generous. She swallowed the tears that she refused to let fall. She'd cried enough over them, and she was done grieving for what she'd never had in the first place. A family. A place to call home. A real one.

'*Bonne nuit*, Beni.'

She tugged the lapels of her jacket around her throat to ward off the chilly autumn breeze now that she wasn't protected by the decorative trees that bordered the roof terrace and stepped away.

How crazy it was to think that once upon a time, she had thought herself in love with a handsome young prince. A real-life prince with a horse and a carriage and a castle to boot.

She gave a choked laugh, mocking herself like all the others, and pressed her fingers to her lips, steadying herself as she checked Beni hadn't noticed.

If he had, he made no show of it as he cleared the table she had used. Her mini sanctum. She didn't have a lot of spaces to hide away in, and whether Beni knew it or not, it really was quite precious. As was the suite she was staying in one floor down. Louis's suite. One of her oldest and dearest friends. One of her *only* friends, if she was honest. Because as she'd swiftly learnt, fame brought out the worst in the best of people; private stories sold in exchange for a price or a royal favour or two.

The crown had cost Cassie her friends, her family, her identity, her financial independence and her freedom, but she was on a mission to take it all back…save for the family and friends. Those that hadn't stuck by her were not worth keeping. But the rest…she'd get there. She would.

She weaved her way through the empty tables and headed for the lift. Too tired to take the stairs. Another good sign that sleep would come easily tonight.

The ornate brass doors welcomed her in, and she stepped inside, stretched out her tired limbs as they closed around her. Breathed in the soothing hotel scent and let it calm her as

the lift slid to a gentle stop on her floor and
the doors opened.

She walked out, head down as she searched
her bag for the key, when something made
her still. A sixth sense, a prickle along her
spine—she was used to having her space invaded when she was out and about, the odd
stalker or excitable fan getting too close and
then security having to intervene. But the
hotel was locked down. No one got to this
floor without a pass, and at this time of night,
there should be no one else around but…

Her lashes lifted, head slow to follow as
her mouth fell open, because there, straight
ahead, was a man. A very tall, very broad,
very *naked* man.

The first thing Hugo became aware of was the
cold. The second was a soft ping. The third was
a gasp. A very horrified, very feminine gasp!

His eyes flared wide. Every sense now alert
as he registered his reflection in the French
windows ahead; his nude silhouette against
the dimmed lights of the Champs-Élysées far
below. And that's when he realised, the ping
was an arriving elevator car and the gasp—
Oh, Mon Dieu!
He spun to face the woman who'd stepped

out of the lift. Dressed in tailored black to her knees, nude tights, classic heels, she stood as regal as a queen…of the haunting, screaming kind!

Her handbag hit the deck as he watched, her belongings spilling free as she pressed her hands to her ghost-like cheeks and the elevator doors slid closed.

'Oh, Mon Dieu!' he repeated aloud, clamping his hands over his front. *'Je suis désolé!'*

Perfectly arched brows disappeared into a sweeping dark fringe, and unthinking, he stepped forward. Her eyes darted down and she stumbled back, one hand blindly reaching for the elevator button. 'Don't come any closer!'

'Pardonnez-moi!' He scanned the hallway, wishing that for all it was opulent and timeless, it had something he could readily use as a shield. He discounted the bronze bust on the console table—too weird. The baroque lamp. It was plugged into the wall. The bin. Just, no. And grabbed an ample-sized vase complete with high-rising white foliage, thrusting it before him as he turned to face her again.

'Please.' He spoke English with her, blowing a stray white frond out of his face. His allergies were *not* going to appreciate this up-close encounter. But they had nothing on her and his nakedness. 'I didn't mean to scare you. I live here.'

Cascading brown waves shimmied with her panicked head shake as she batted the button, which seemed to be having no effect whatsoever. Was she even hitting it? He'd be taking *that* up with hotel maintenance come morning…

'I *do*,' he stressed, focusing on more pressing concerns—panicked hotel guest versus his indecent exposure. 'Just here!'

He nudged his head in the direction of his very closed, very *locked* penthouse door.

He swallowed a curse. 'And it appears, I am now locked out.'

She eyed the door, her hand ceasing its attack on the elevator button as she lifted it to the pearls around her neck. Did she think he was going to rob her? A naked robber? Was that a thing?

He shuddered and hurried to explain. 'I know this looks bad. And I'm not making this up. I sleepwalk. And just now, as far as I knew it, I was stepping into a cab, going who knows where with who knows who, when the elevator went ping and you gasped and I came to. I *swear* it.'

The fear in her big round eyes eased a fraction. He couldn't make out their colour in the low light favoured by his hotels at night, only that her perfectly applied makeup accentuated their alluring shape and size…the kind a man could readily lose his mind in.

And yes, he had to be half asleep if *that's* the thought he was entertaining while the chilling draft from the ancient glass continued to assault his very exposed ass.

'Then why haven't I seen you before?' She gifted him the side eye with a hint of fire. *Hallelujah.*

'I've been away on business for the past month. I got back a few hours ago. You can call Vincent on the front desk. He'll confirm it. In fact, *do* call Vincent because I don't have a key on my naked person and I really don't want to terrorise the rest of the building by going down there like this. Terrorising one hotel guest is enough, and as I own the place, it really won't look good for business.'

Her mouth twitched. The pink glossy shape pulling back into one dimpled cheek, a hint of colour creeping in—*Dieu merci!*

'You own the place?'

'This and many others. *Oui.*'

'You are Chevalier of Chevalier Clubs?'

'I know, yes. It's very original. I've heard it all before. '

She laughed softly and *damn* if the sound didn't warm him all the more. He needed more of that.

'I'm just relieved I can trust you to be well behaved while I call in the cavalry, Mr Chevalier.'

'You can call me Hugo. I think we're long past the need for surnames here…'

She didn't comment as she dipped to the floor, not once taking her eyes from his as the elevator doors eased open behind her. He half expected her to scurry back inside and get the hell away while awaiting said cavalry. But she didn't. She swept up her belongings, dropping all but her phone back inside her bag.

He was right about her regal air. Every movement was so carefully poised, the way her knees stayed pressed together, her head remained high, her shoulders held back. There was something about her too. Something familiar…achingly so…

Or was it just the late hour, the hazy remnants of his dream messing with his head? His memories? The warped world between reality and make-believe…because if he'd met her before, surely, he'd have remembered her name at least.

And what was a woman like her doing wandering the halls of the hotel at such a late hour, or early, depending on how one looked at it. Alone too?

She looked like she'd been to dinner, or the theatre, a function perhaps. Her appearance *too* pristine to be doing the walk of shame. Too composed to—

And what are you even doing debating her presence when you're the one stood in the public corridor? Butt! Naked!

He watched as she dialled the front desk, her elegant long fingers making light work of the task before her eyes returned to his. Her gaze thankfully more bemused now as she lifted the phone to her ear and Hugo rocked on his feet. Wondered where to look. As first meetings went, this had to be up there with the most embarrassing, most memorable…

And still, the question remained. There were only two penthouse suites on this floor. His and Louis Cousteau's. And she wasn't Louis's type. Wrong sex for a start.

'Vincent, c'est Cassie…'

Cassie. The name softened her somewhat. Made her more…accessible. He listened as she spoke to his night porter. Her French seeming to come easy, though there was an awkward stumble when she got to the state of his…he cleared his throat…undress.

Hugo pulled his shoulders back as a shiver threatened to roll through him. He couldn't do much about the head-to-toe goose-bumps, though, or the rapidly shrivelling… *Oh, dear*. Throat clearing could be quite habit forming— who knew?

'He's on his way.'

She slotted the phone into her bag and Hugo gave an abrupt nod, which in turn sent the floral fronds right up his nose. He scrunched his face up, battling a sneeze, battling it… battling it—

'A-Achoo!'

She flinched. 'Bless you.'

'I'm sorry!' He turned his head to the side, swallowed another. 'Allergies.'

'Oh, dear, perhaps flowers weren't the best choice of a shield.'

'Short of pulling the lamp out of the wall, I didn't have much choice.'

She looked around too and then stepped forward, shrugging out of her jacket as she went. 'Here.'

Now he was the one taking a back step. 'I couldn't possibly.'

There was no way on earth he was going to put her clothing anywhere near his—

'It's fine.'

She was a stride away, jacket held out, decorative vase the only thing keeping her from getting another eyeful. This time, up close and personal.

Maybe he should install coat stands complete with coats throughout his hotels for such random eventualities in future…hell, he'd settle for an umbrella!

'I promise not to look…' she said, her eyes meeting his as her delicate little throat gave a delicate little bob '…not again anyway.'

What on earth was she doing?

The only man she'd ever seen naked in all her adult years was her ex, the Prince. But if anyone deserved to wear the title visually, it was this man.

He was a solid wall of muscle. Tall. Broad. Fierce. And she would have said Eastern European, but his accent was all French. Thick and seductive and…and she really should have stopped at one martini.

She turned her head away, eyes averted as

her skin prickled and warmed. Every millimetre aware of him being so very close. So very close and so very naked.

'Are you sure?'

She nodded, not trusting her voice.

And as he moved, the air shifted between them. Her senses strained. The soft clink of the vase against the marble ridiculously loud as he returned it to the side. The heat of his fingers sweeping like fire against hers as he took her jacket from her outstretched hands. His scent invaded her nostrils. He'd showered recently. He smelled clean, masculine, and her head…her head was busy visualising far too much. The reflection in the gold elevator doors, distorted, but revealing enough. Especially when her memory was all too willing to fill in the blanks.

'Thank you, Cassie.'

Her lips parted with her breath. To have a stranger address her by name…it had been too long. Louis still called her Cassie. Always had. Always would. They'd been friends long before the crown. But this man…this Hugo Chevalier. She wanted to kiss him. *Not* a good idea.

She opted for a much safer smile, turning

back to him as she secured her arms around her middle. 'You're welcome.'

'But now you're cold...'

He gestured with one shoulder as he tied her jacket around his waist, his brow furrowed in concern as he took in her bare arms and tight grip. Her clenched jaw likely too.

'I'm fine.'

She tried to keep her eyes level with his, but this close she could see every exquisite detail of his face...and the man was, well, he was bewitching. Maybe there was something mystical to this whole witching hour after all, because she was losing her ability to think straight.

From his dark cropped hair with the slightest peak that gave him a heart-shaped brow... a kind brow. To his dark eyebrows that arched over eyes that spoke of a strength, a steeliness, but also a sweetness...and how was that even possible? They could be grey or blue. It was hard to tell in the low light of the hall.

He had a kind nose too—straight and smooth. And a mouth that softened into a smile that made her stomach turn to goo. The dark stubble that bracketed his mouth and followed the sharp cut of jaw seemed suave and deliberate. The man *liked* to look good. *Knew* he looked good. Just like Georges. Which should put her on edge.

But how could she be on edge when he was the one naked and locked out, her tiny jacket his only protection…

'I think it looks better on you,' she murmured, a teasing quirk to her lips.

He chuckled, his pecs giving a delightful ripple that had her palms tingling against her arms.

'Once again, I do apologise. I'm sure this is the last thing you wanted to come home to.'

'You're just lucky it's me and not Louis. I don't think he would have been so kind as to offer out any form of a shield.'

'Louis is a friend of yours?'

'*Oui*. He's kindly gifted me his place until I…' Her gaze drifted to the Champs-Élysées beyond the glass as her thoughts drifted to her unpleasant reality and she beat them back. 'Until I can find myself a more permanent home.'

With a career that she had yet to get off the ground…

'Are you looking to stay in Paris?'

She frowned at him. Did he really not recognise her?

At first, she'd been too stunned by his nakedness to think about him recognising her. Then she'd been too caught up in getting him covered up. But with him calling her 'Cassie' and the continued ease? An ease that shouldn't really exist. He was still very much naked, and her jacket wasn't covering all that much. And seriously, those abs and those legs…they looked like they could crack a—

'Cassie?'

Gulp. She tugged her gaze back to his. *'Pardonnez-moi.'* She really wasn't used to such a fine specimen of a man this close and this naked. 'What were you saying?'

His eyes lit with something—something she wasn't all too sure she should be identifying with. 'I was asking if you're looking to stay in Paris?'

'I'm looking to stay in…' she repeated dumbly, wondering if she could stay a whole lot longer if these were the kind of encounters she might experience with the owner of her current abode…which was a wholly inappropriate thought to be having. Once again, she blamed Beni's excellent martinis.

And thank heaven for the ping of the elevator at that precise moment.

She sprang back. 'Vincent!'

Hugo's mouth, a rather deliciously full mouth

for a man, quirked to the left and flashed a dimple. 'Funny place that…?'

'I should let you get back to your bed.' She backed up, all the way to Louis's door, scrambling for the key in her handbag. 'I hope your sleep is much more restful from here on out, Mr Chevalier.'

'Wait! Your jacket…'

She waved him away—*oh, God no*—eyes anywhere but on him as she fumbled over the lock. Telling Vincent the situation over the phone was one thing, having Vincent *witness* the ex-Princess of Sérignone in a deserted hallway with the naked hotelier, aka his boss, was something else.

Especially with the flush of colour she was now sporting from the chest up.

The door finally sprang open and she sprang in.

'Goodnight, Mr Chevalier. Sweet dreams!'

Because she was sure to have plenty.

Though perhaps *sweet* was the wrong descriptor for the hot and tangled mess of Cassie's sheets that night…

CHAPTER TWO

THE NEXT MORNING Hugo knocked on Louis's door, rolled his shoulders back and waited.

He was sure she was in. The floorboards in the old building gave enough groans away to indicate that someone was home…and that was without him being extra sensitive to her presence following their impromptu encounter.

He eyed the flowers in one hand, her dry-cleaned jacket in his other. The former, an apology he'd had sourced from his favoured florist early that morning. The latter, hers to return.

He didn't want to leave them on her doorstep like some coward. He didn't want her to think him too embarrassed to say hello. Even if the smallest wriggle in his gut told him there might be some of that going on.

He'd never been so quick to escape Vincent's presence as the night before. Though his concierge had handled his state of undress remarkably well, he wasn't ready to be reminded of it just yet. And though he was sure his concierge hadn't shared the news around his staff, Hugo hadn't done his morning rounds as was his usual way upon his return. He'd simply requested that the bouquet be sent up and left it at that.

Besides, he had more pressing matters to attend to. Like a personal apology to deliver now that he was in full possession of his faculties and his clothing.

The elevator pinged and his cheeks heated as he relived Cassie's arrival… Okay, so the embarrassment was still there. But, *Dieu*, it was hardly ideal meeting anyone for the first time in one's birthday suit. Only your parents should get that privilege, and even then…

The elevator opened and the cleaning trolley emerged with two members of staff. One he recognised, one he didn't. Must be new. He sent a polite smile in their general direction and went back to his business while they went about theirs. Clearing his throat, he knocked again.

This time he heard footsteps on the other side. Slow but coming closer. They paused and his senses came alive, awareness prickling as she eyed him through the peephole. An eternity seemed to pass. Was he going to have to explain his presence through a… *closed door*?

Click. The lock turned. The door eased open a crack and one eye peeked out. Vibrant and green. *Sans* makeup today too.

'Mr Chevalier?' She seemed to breathe his name, the delicate sound doing something weird to his chest and that ring of familiarity upped a notch. 'What are you doing here?'

'Good morning.' He tried for a smile, feeling oddly unnerved. Was it the familiarity or the fact that she wasn't exactly welcoming?

Well, would you be after seeing you *naked?*

'I come bearing a gift as an apology and one freshly laundered jacket.'

He lifted both items into view and a delightful flush filled her cheek. He caught the hint of a smile too.

'You really didn't need to do that.'

'I must confess, *I* didn't. I had my staff do it for me.'

'But you would've missed housekeeping for this morning…'

'There have to be some perks to owning a hotel.'

The door eased a little wider, as did her smile,

and his shoulders eased from their surprising position around his ears.

'That is most kind.' She reached out for the jacket and her oversized cream sweater slid down her bare shoulder. She hurried to tug it back up, her blush deepening. 'You really needn't have troubled yourself further.'

She was looking at the flowers as she tucked the jacket to her chin. Eyeing him beneath her lashes as though she was shy. *Was* she shy? Hell, he'd been the naked one, but then maybe she was still *seeing* him naked. *Mon Dieu.*

Until he could bury that image, she would likely keep seeing him so.

'Here, please.' He offered the bouquet of classic cream buds, which she took, her green eyes lighting up as she brought them to her nose.

'Hydrangeas?'

'I put in a special request for a hypoallergenic variety.' He gave her a lopsided grin and cocked his head towards the floral display that had been his protection a few hours ago. 'And I'm now considering that for the health of all my guests, I should have these evil varieties replaced throughout.'

Her eyes danced. 'Hydrangeas certainly would have hidden a lot more.'

She was warming up. And her teasing had him warming from the inside out too, which encouraged him enough to say, 'Can I tempt you to a coffee? There's a barista down the road that the tourists have yet to discover, and I'd love to...'

His invitation trailed off as the colour drained from her face. Had he dropped his pants unawares again, because now she was back to being aghast? Not quite the screaming, Hail Mary affair of the night before, but pale, nonetheless.

'What's wrong?'

And truth was he hadn't *meant* to invite her for coffee. It hadn't been his intention at all when he'd come here. But he didn't feel in any hurry to leave her orbit. Not after the week he'd just endured with his parents in LA. His father had refused to stick to his retirement plan and keep his nose out of the global security business he'd set up forty years ago...a business that would take his dying breath if he let it.

Only, Hugo hadn't thought of his father and his firm since Cassie had stunned him awake.

And today was Saturday, the weekend for

most. Not that he had treated it as such in a long time. Especially since he'd rolled his father's business into his ever-expanding list of responsibilities.

But now he was taking a moment to think about it, it was the perfect excuse for a leisurely coffee with a companion who certainly looked like she was enjoying her own chilled-out weekend. Her jumper having resumed its slouched position off one shoulder, her soft grey leggings and fluffy white socks designed for lounging, her hair hanging free and tousled to her waist…

He could feel another throat clearing coming on, and what was that about?

You really need to ask?

'Nothing. I'm—' She licked her lips. 'I'm not dressed to go out.'

'I'm talking coffee, not cocktails at the Ritz.' He was hoping to reassure her, to tease a little too. Surely she had to know how good she looked? Sweet and cute, in a sexy girl-next-door kind of a way. But her smile remained weak.

'I should get these in some water.'

'Of course.'

She eased away from the door and a chill washed over his front. Disappointment wrapped up in that same sense of familiarity—ringing stronger, resonating deeper. But then, he'd walked many a hotel corridor, attended many a black tie affair, met many, many people over the years. Though it was more than how she looked. It was the way she was. The regal air. The shyness. The sweetness and light.

'I'll leave you to get on with your day.'

He turned on his heel and moved off, cursing the disappointed burr to his voice. It wasn't in his nature to guilt trip people. Problem was, he *was* disappointed, and it had taken him by surprise.

'Mr Chevalier…'

He paused, angled his head just enough to say, 'Hugo, please.'

'Would you like to come in for coffee?'

His brows drew together—was she just being kind, polite…?

'I was about to have one myself,' she added as though sensing his hesitation.

'So long as I'm not keeping you from whatever you had planned for today?'

'Not at all. To be honest, it would be nice to have some company.'

His frown lifted. 'You're sure?'

She stepped back to make room for him to enter. 'Though I don't know how well you know Louis or if you've been in here since he took ownership of the apartment, but…'

Her voice trailed away as she let the space speak for itself, which it did, a thousand times over as he crossed the threshold and chuckled. 'I believe one's home should always be a reflection of the occupant's personality, and since this is Louis's and Louis Cousteau is a flamboyant fashion designer, I think it is perfection.'

The twinkle in her eye was worth every eye-watering item adorning the large entrance hall. 'That's one word for it.'

He and Louis's penthouse suites were of a similar size and layout, but there the similarity ended. Statement pieces, whether it be in colour or shape, personality or origin, filled every wall, every space. And if Hugo was honest, it gave him the twinge of a headache, but who was he to judge? He was a minimalist through and through. Everything in his life had been about pleasing others, or at the very least, avoiding offence.

The same could not be said for the great Louis Cousteau.

'You do get used to it after a while.'

She was at the glitter-bedazzled sink, in

the equally bedazzled kitchen, filling a vase with water.

'I'm saying nothing.'

She smiled. 'You didn't need to.' Sparkling green eyes went back to the vase as she arranged the flowers within it. 'Louis was never one for toeing a line of any sort.'

'A trait I can admire.'

And he did. That was no lie.

Hugo had grown up in a household at war… whenever his father was at home at any rate. He'd been trying to find the line to toe forever, and then beseeching everyone else to toe it too. He'd been the doting son, the people-pleaser, the peace facilitator in his parents' marriage, where there had always been three according to his mother—her, his father, and the company.

Not any more, though… *Retired*, remember.

If only his father would get the message and leave well alone.

'Is filter coffee, okay?' The hesitation in her voice already had him giving a smile in reassurance—*see*, people-pleaser. Even though he'd long ago left that boy behind, some habits were harder to shift. 'Or I can try and master the machine?'

He looked at the contraption against one wall, too shiny and new to have ever been used. 'A filter is perfect.'

And if he was honest, he liked his coffee by the vat. He might be French—well, Polish if one wanted to go a generation back, but he'd take a giant mug over a measly espresso cup any day of the week.

He entered the living space, leaving her to get the coffee going. He got the impression she didn't entertain often. Which again was strange, considering how she'd appeared the night before. How sophisticated, elegant, and dressed for entertaining.

Or was it that he'd been the complete opposite, so unprepared for company?

No. He didn't think it was that. More that she was used to being waited on. And unaccustomed to entertaining anybody when dressed so casually. But if he was honest, he liked her like this.

Even if she did stand out against the backdrop, her hesitation and muted presence against the garish backdrop a bit like setting a skittish kitten down in a neon nightclub. Maybe he should have invited her round to his place…she'd have fit right in with all the monochrome and he could have taken care of the coffee. Though he'd need to put a few coffees between them and his nakedness before that could happen!

He followed the criss-crossed panels of sun coming through the many French windows and doors to the low-slung coffee table that was scattered with drawing paraphernalia. Pencils, pens, sketches of clothing and accessories...

'Please excuse the mess.'

He turned to find her behind him.

'Louis left it like this?'

The man didn't strike him as the kind to leave stuff just lying around. Chaotic but not messy. Especially when such designs were obviously in their early stages and likely to be considered top secret. His cleaning staff could be trusted but...

She coloured, swept her hair behind her ear. 'No, they're mine.'

'*Yours?* Wow, they're really—' He was about to say *impressive*, but she was already hurrying forward, gathering the sheets into a pile. Did she not want him to see? Was she self-conscious? Or was it as he thought...

'Top secret?'

'What?' She straightened with a laugh, clutching the drawings to her chest. 'Hardly.

Not really. They're—they're just some designs I've been working on.'

'Do you work with Louis? Is that how you two know each another?'

'Not officially, no. We've known each other for a long time. We went to school together in London.'

She stacked the papers on a side table shaped like a palm tree and gestured for him to take a seat on the velvet sofa, the colour of which made him wince but the fabric was soft enough. He swung an arm across its back, was about to ask her which school when his gaze landed on the pile of magazines her cleared-away sketches had unveiled.

Or rather, landed on the cover model of the top magazine…

The cover model who then took a seat beside him in the flesh.

'Yes,' she said, and he started. 'That's me.'

No, he couldn't have been so unaware, so sucker-punched by their first encounter that he'd missed…missed…

He blinked and turned to face her, eyes widening and seeing every detail anew. The green eyes. The dark hair. The petite frame. He thought of the recognition that had been nagging at him. The familiarity. The poised elegance with the touch of shyness—something thousands if not millions adored, and others questioned.

Cassie was Cassandra, Princess of Sérignone. *Ex* Princess.

English socialite. A woman of the people. A woman whose recent divorce was the talk of the world's media, and there he'd been… naked…unawares…how stupid she must think him!

'Mr Chevalier?'

Though he hadn't been in his right mind. And it had been dark in the outer hall. And even this morning, he'd been too concerned with making right what he had made wrong. And then she'd been all shy and sweet and…

Princess *Freaking* Cassandra?

He dragged a hand down his face.

'I'm sorry. I didn't realise.'

He contemplated standing. *Dieu*, he contemplated bowing, but it all felt a little late for that.

She gave him a coy smile. *That* smile.

'I know. And I wasn't quite sure how to tell you.'

'I would bow but…'

Her eyes danced, her thoughts travelling all

the way to his naked backside and beyond, he was sure…

'So, you're the reason for the extra foot-fall outside when I arrived home yesterday? I'd assumed we were having an out-of-season flurry of tourists.'

She grimaced. 'Mostly press I'm afraid. I'm sorry.'

'Why are you sorry?'

'For bringing the madness to your door, to your hotel.'

'Considering I brought you my nakedness, I think we can call it even, don't you?'

She gave him a full-on smile. The beam of which made him lose his breath. *Breath-taking*. It was a word he'd heard of, knew of, never once had he deemed it fit for another person. A hard run, a spell in the boxing ring, a blast round the Nürburgring. But never about a woman.

And that's when it hit him. The nagging recognition, the stirring in his gut—it wasn't because she was Cassandra, Princess of Sérignone. It was that she reminded him of another woman. Another dark-haired, shy yet teasing woman. She reminded him of Sara. Of his past and his one big mistake.

Ice rushed his veins, goose-bumps prickling against the sleeves of his shirt.

'Your hotel security have been amazing, Mr Chevalier, but I am sorry for the extra work I'm putting them through.'

He swallowed the chilling boulder that had lodged itself in his chest. 'We're an exclusive hotel, we deal with clients that require extra security all the time. It's their job to handle it.'

'Still…'

She looked hesitant, and he knew his tension had seeped into his words. He cursed the memories for rearing their ugly head. It was ancient history. Over a decade old. He'd not thought of Sara in so long. She had cost him dearly in so many ways. She wasn't just the woman he'd thought himself in love with, she was the woman who'd lost him his father's respect, his first career, almost his life as well as hers…back when he'd been a rookie bodyguard.

A bodyguard who should have known better than to fall in love with his principal.

It's why he kept a tight hold on his emotions now. Especially when it came to people. He didn't depend on them to give him a rush of any kind.

Now he was thirty-six, a billionaire hotelier

with a finger in the pie that was his father's global security firm. The biggest lesson he'd learnt was that you couldn't control what others thought or did or felt. They would go the way they wanted. And it was best to disassociate your own happiness, your own feelings, from those of others.

Which left him all the more disturbed now, because he cared about this woman. This woman who was no more than a stranger to him personally, but he'd seen enough in the press to know her life had to be some kind of living hell of late. Her divorce as loud and as messy as a catastrophic world event. He wasn't one for reading the gossip columns, but she often featured in the mainstream headlines. People picking and probing into her personal life like they had every right.

'I'm sorry you're under such attack, but if my hotel and my staff are helping you to feel safe from their prying presence, then that's as good as any five-star review for me.'

Her eyes warmed with his words. 'Are you going to ask if any of it is true?'

'If any of what is true?'

'I don't know—take your pick. People usually have their favourite headline…corrupt-

ing the son of my ex-husband's driver seems
to be the latest story.'

'You're confusing me with someone who
cares, Cassie.'

To anyone else, his remark may have caused
offence. Instead she positively bloomed and,
in her warmth, the chill within him eased.

'It really is none of my business, unless of
course you would appreciate a friendly ear.'

Her lashes flickered, her green eyes sig-
nalling something that he couldn't read but
it had the unease returning—the familiarity,
the need to protect, the urge to run and stay
at the same time.

'Anyway…' He shifted back in his seat, creating an extra inch between them like it would
somehow release the weird hold she had over
him. 'The extra income from the reporters
staying and dining here will be good for business, but if one crosses the line, you only have
to say the word and they're out. Though to
give them their due, they all seemed rather
well-behaved upon my arrival.'

'That's because it was you in their orbit.'
And not her.
She didn't need to say it for him to know
that's what she meant. And there was so much
in that one statement. So much vehemence, so

much power that she had bestowed on them—the press—and so much fear. Just like Sara.

He opened his mouth to reassure, to tell her she was safe in his building, to tell her he'd evict them all, if need be, when she stood. 'I'll get the coffee.'

He doubted the pot would be ready but he got the impression she wanted a breather more than the drink, and so he let her go. It could wait.

And if he was honest, he could do with a breather too.

It wasn't so much that she was royalty—*ex*-royalty. He'd protected royalty. He'd housed royalty. Hell, he'd *dated* the equivalent of royalty. And there came Sara again.

'You know what your problem is, son? You've got a thing for a damsel in distress, and until you can keep a lid on it, you're no use to me...'

His father's decade-old words were in his ear, his disappointed gaze in his head too... didn't matter that it didn't apply now. That his father's grave dismissal had no place in the now.

His career was his own. His money was his own. His life was his own.

But the damsel in distress, was that what this was…? Sara. Cassie. Both damsels of a sort?

He shook off the thought, dismissed it even as it tried to come back at him…history on repeat just in another form.

But if it was a case of history repeating itself, didn't that mean he had a chance to rewrite the ending and come out the hero this time? Could he help Cassie get through this turbulent time in her life and not play himself for a lovesick fool, because this time he wouldn't *be* a lovesick fool.

Cassie brought the tray back into the lounge. She couldn't tell if Hugo Chevalier had a sweet tooth. Her gut told her not. Or rather, his well-toned physique did, but she brought the brass pineapple sugar pot anyway. More because it made her smile.

He started to rise. 'Let me help you with that.'

'No need.' She set the tray down, careful not to spill a drop from the two steaming mugs filled with coffee or the jug of milk. 'Despite the rumours, a princess can manage to serve her own coffee…'

And brush her hair, cleanse her face, clothe herself…*how novel*!

He settled back into his seat. 'Do you have to do that a lot? Justify what you can and can't do, fend off the would-be waiting staff?'

She didn't meet his eye. She already felt like he'd leapt inside her head, read her every thought as she'd had it. Not that there were any staff waiting in the wings here. Not any more.

It didn't stop the learned response though— the slight tension in her spine, an attuned ear, and the tight lip, which she swiftly loosened into a smile for his benefit.

'Once upon a time, in a castle far, far away…' She handed him his mug and he thanked her, his gaze flitting to the exposed skin of her shoulder, and she fought the urge to cover it as her cheeks heated. She was dressed for comfort, not for company. A fact she'd tried to point out when he'd made the joke about the Ritz. But there was being dressed for the Ritz and being dressed like she was. Braless and in her comfiest clothes. Her go-to outfit after a morning's workout, when all she'd planned to do was to block the noise of the world out and let her creative juices take over.

'But not any more?'

'No.' She sank back into the sofa, curled her

legs up under her. 'Now I get to make my own coffee. When I want, how I want, and drink it with who I want.'

'And this is a good thing, right? Because from where I'm sitting, there seems to be some unresolved tension about the whole situation.'

Her eyes shot to his. Had he really just gone there? Outed her and her 'situation' again without a moment's hesitation? She gave a grimace. 'Did it really come across like that?'

'A little.'

'Sorry. I'm not very good at this.'

'Good at what exactly? The coffee. The talking. Or…'

'The company.'

'Am I that hard to be around?' But his eyes danced with the question, the soft curve to his lips telling her he hadn't taken offence, and he didn't mean any.

She laughed, the tension between her shoulder blades easing with every ripple. What was it about this man that made her feel almost normal. 'Not at all. Just…different.'

'Different?'

'To be honest, a coffee date of any kind is a new one on me. Even with Louis it's usually a glitzy affair that revolves around fashion and dogs.'

He cocked a brow. 'Dogs?'

'Oh, yes, he *loves* dogs.'

'I can *try* and talk fashion and dogs if that'll make you feel more comfortable, but I can't make any promises about how riveting it'll be. Or accurate. I can do colour, size, maybe the odd name drop, but that's my lot.'

'I take it you have people who pick out your clothing then, because for one who claims to have little knowledge of fashion, you clearly have an eye for it?'

'Is that a roundabout way of complimenting me on how I dress, Cassie?'

Her cheeks warmed and his eyes dipped, taking in the flush that must have risen up her chest, too. Oh, dear. She was so out of practice and very bad at this. 'It was merely an observation, Mr Chevalier.'

'Now that we're enjoying coffee together, do you think you could drop the Mr? Especially since technically if anyone should be giving anyone a rank, it's me to you.'

Her coffee threatened to escape her mug as she thrust her hand out. 'Please don't!'

He raised that same arrogant brow.

'I've been called *princess* enough to last

one lifetime, and I know that probably sounds ungrateful when it's many a young girl's dream but...'

She shuddered. She hadn't meant to, but the chilling memories creeping along her spine were impossible to suppress.

'Let me guess, the reality isn't all it's cracked up to be?'

'No.'

He captured her gaze in his. The warmth, the understanding in his crystal-clear blue eyes choked up her chest and had the words spilling forth before she could stop them, 'It's more prisoner than princess.'

She bit her lip. Shocked at what she'd said. Because she knew full well how that line would be printed in the press. How it would look to the world when shown in black and white and worse still, it would be the truth. Because she *had* said it.

And she didn't know Hugo from Adam. How could she trust him not to spill all when he left here? To sell her story like so many others had before. Her nearest and dearest, people she'd once thought of as friends. 'I shouldn't have said that.'

She clamped her teeth down again so hard she thought she might draw blood, because the truth was, she wanted to talk to him. The urge like an ever-swelling tide within her. She couldn't explain it. She'd had no one for so long. Not even Louis would sit quietly, calmly, and listen like this. Oh, he was a good friend, so long as it was surface level talk. The practical or financial. Designs and creative fun. But this…the deep, emotional, real.

There was just something about Hugo. Something that told her he understood. That he got it.

'It's okay, Cassie. You can trust me.'

He lowered his mug to the table, rested his elbows on his knees as he interlaced his fingers and gave her his full attention.

'I don't make a habit of gossiping, and I certainly don't talk to reporters, and in all honesty, the idea that *you* could go outside and tell the world that you found me wandering one of my hotels in my birthday suit fills *me* with dread.'

A streak of pink marred his cheeks and she found it endearing. Both the blush and the honesty.

'That aside, it would hardly look good for business if I were to go about selling stories on my guests. And in case you need it spelled out, I really don't need the cash or the press attention.'

There was no arrogance, just fact.

'So, if you keep my secrets, I'll keep yours. How does that sound?'

'*Très bien*, Hugo,' she said, and with all her heart, she meant it too. 'I agree.'

CHAPTER THREE

'So, a prisoner, you say? How so?'

Though he could take a wild guess. Not so wild if he was to think of Sara and her life as the daughter of a head of state. Her father may have been the figurehead, but the rules and expectations very much applied to her. Governing what she could and couldn't do. Where she could and couldn't go. Who she could and couldn't see. Who she could and couldn't *date*. Him.

'Where do I even start?'

He settled back into the sofa, making clear he had all the time in the world to listen. 'Why not start at the beginning, it's as good a place as any…'

She sipped at her coffee, her mouth twisting around the mug. 'You might regret saying that, Hugo.'

He waved a hand through the air. 'Feel free to remind me later.'

She gave a soft huff, the returning shadows in her green eyes chasing away the amusement and making him want to close the gap between them. But he also sensed the persistent skittishness about her, the wary kitten-like quality he'd spied earlier.

'If I'm honest, I never had freedom like other kids growing up, so it wasn't like I could miss it. My parents had my life mapped out from birth. Every step was strategic and they played me to their best advantage.'

He gave a slow nod. 'That sounds…'

'Militant?'

'Exhausting.'

She blew out a breath. 'That too. But the palace was different. Every day had a schedule. Breakfast, lunch, dinner. You name it. There was a time for it and someone would produce it. And if you were especially lucky, there'd be a different outfit for each.'

'Where my family comes from in Poland, such abundance would be severely frowned upon.'

'You're from Poland—I thought so.' Her smile made a return. Bright, genuine. 'And I would agree with them all. And I said as much to the King. Who was of course horrified, as was his mother. I was quickly shushed and escorted from the room by Georges and told never to give my opinion in public, or private, again.'

'How lovely.'

'Quite.'

'What are they like? Really?'

'His family?' Her eyes flashed and her nose flared. 'The King is a brute. His wife is a spendthrift. And while the Queen Mother despairs at their behaviour, his son runs amok. If I was to be kind, I would say the King is angry at the world for daring to mock his virility. His wife spends to make up for the abundance of children she so desperately wanted. His mother despairs at her lack of power, and as for Georges, well, the apple doesn't fall far from the tree…after five years of marriage I failed to provide even one heir.'

His gut clenched. 'So, he divorced *you*?'

'God, no. I divorced him. When I realised I was the only one who took our wedding vows seriously.'

His shoulders eased as he released a breath he hadn't noticed he was holding.

'I'd had enough of the real Georges and everyone laughing at me behind closed doors. I think he shares the worst qualities of both his mother and his father, and now he can share those qualities with whomever he chooses, as I no longer need to care because I'm no longer there to witness it.'

Hugo shook his head, unable to understand how she'd been able to bear it for so long and still hold her head as high as she did. All that poise and elegance, she had it in spades. She hadn't lost it. Georges hadn't stolen it. No matter how the palace had tried.

'And so, they sow seeds of twisted dealings and affairs on your part, suggesting it was *your* unfaithful behaviour that led to the breakdown of your marriage? Despite all the stories that have been in the media over the years about him?'

She gave a sad smile. 'I know.'

'But how do you stand it? All the slander being thrown at you.'

'I ignore it as best I can. I made my bed. I knew who he was when I agreed to marry him. I knew of his reputation, but I thought I'd done the unthinkable and reformed the playboy prince. Though even I hadn't known just how much there was to reform when my parents presented our engagement as a fait accompli.'

'But surely you had a choice, you could have said no?'

She gave a tight laugh. 'One does not say no to my parents.'

'Why?'

'I'd lived a life doing what was expected of me and so I did it.' She tilted her head at him. Green eyes probing as they scanned him from top to toe. 'Call it fear, impotence, apathy... I can't imagine someone like you knowing what it means to live like that.'

He shifted under that gaze because he'd felt it all. Once. Feared for his life. Watched the woman he'd believed in walk away, powerless to stop her. And when his father had stripped him of his role in the company, he hadn't cared. He'd only vowed never to feel any of those things again.

'Did you ever rebel, even when you were younger? There must have been times...?'

She caught her lip in her teeth as her eyes drifted to the coffee table. 'When I was seven, my mother bought me a dress to wear to a summer function. I hated it. It itched like crazy, making my skin red raw, and I refused to wear it. She locked me in the basement and left me there in the dark. Told me I could come out when I had the dress on. The party was two days later...'

He waited for the punch line and when nothing came, he realised that was it.

'She came and got you…'

She nodded. 'Yes. Two days later. The staff fed me scraps but she saw to it that my hair was scraped up, my blotchy cheeks were well covered, and I smiled until my face ached.'

He felt the bite of his nails in his palm and flexed his fist. 'Some parenting technique.'

'Mind games were always my mother's way.'

'Dare I ask about your father's?'

'My father was all about the purse strings and the silent treatment. It could have been worse.'

And he'd been thinking worse. Now he felt bad to be relieved!

'I often wondered if it would have been easier if I had had a sister or a brother to love and to share the load a little, but I think that would have made it worse. I would have worried about them too.'

He could believe it.

'And the truth is, I *was* the one who said yes to the marriage. I met the Prince and he— he charmed me. Georges was good at making you believe what he said. He had these dreamy blue eyes and this compelling smile.

And I'd been so caught up in his flattery, his attention, his *kindness*. He gave me everything I'd been starved of as a child. While my friends were all craving sweets, chocolate, the kind of treats Mum would never permit, all I'd wanted was love, a kind word, cuddles...' She gave a shaky laugh, her cheeks blooming with colour that killed him now. 'God, I sound pathetic.'

'No. No, you don't. *They* do. Your parents. Georges. His family. The whole lot of them.'

Hell, he wanted to storm the castle and hold them all to account.

'He made me feel special, and I—I was swept up in it all. I thought we were falling in love and so I married him. I believed our own love story. *The English Socialite who had snagged the Playboy Prince.*'

Her green eyes misted over, her thoughts travelling back in time as she relived those early days. 'I didn't realise I was being played for a fool until it was too late. My father had saved the royal reserves with Fairfax money and I was Princess of Sérignone. There was no going back...until I couldn't take it any more.'

He studied her quietly, admiring the strength it must have taken to walk away, to *stay* away.

'And what about your parents now? Where are they?'

'At home in England, last I checked.'

'Have you…'

'Have I spoken to them? Oh, yes, they were my first port of call when I ran from the palace. I'm not sure why I thought they would shelter me, but what choice did I have? A princess doesn't really have many friends they can trust, and I figured they wouldn't want me roaming the streets stirring up ever more trouble…'

'But?'

'My mother tried to talk me into returning—like I said, mind games are her speciality—while my father physically escorted me to his private jet back to Sérignoné.'

'Your own father?'

'*Oui*. So you see, I am done with them, Hugo. Since then, the few friends I have left have helped me by giving me places to stay while I build up my portfolio, in the hope that soon, I'll have enough to launch a career in fashion and become financially independent once more. Then I can pay back all those people like Louis who have helped me get here and I can also get back to my charity work that I have missed so much.'

He shook his head. 'I can't believe that you're here, fighting to take your life back and already thinking about giving back to others.'

She gave him a lopsided smile. 'I'm sickening, I know.'

'Is that what Georges would tell you?' Because he wasn't seeing the funny side.

Her eyes widened. 'How did you...?'

'Something tells me that that man and his family tried to stamp out every good thing about you so that it may make him shine that little bit brighter.'

'Funny you say that.'

'How so?'

'Because after our marriage it often occurred to me that it wasn't just the Fairfax money the Duponts were after, but my 'clean' image too. I was a way to mop up the mess that Georges was making with his wild and hedonistic parties. *Now*, if I'd known about *those* at the time of our engagement then I might have been more reluctant to trot down that aisle...'

Hugo didn't think he could take much of the Georges revelation train, or rather, his teeth couldn't. 'Seems to me the Duponts got plenty out of the marriage, and I can see how you were duped, but what I don't understand is what your parents got in return?'

'Status. Royal connections. Another boost for the family tree? I don't know and I don't want to know. Unpacking that only leads to me understanding my true worth to them, and I'm not sure I want to know that. Whereas I do know that I want a fresh start and a clean slate so that I can focus on my future free of them all.'

She gave a smile and, cupping her mug in both hands, she retreated further into the sofa. He knew the mug was giving her the warmth her body lacked. The sofa, the comfort. And he had the deep-rooted urge to provide both.

'And heaven knows there are people in this world who are starving, who don't have a roof over their head, live under threat each day with zero hope of change. People who I want to get my life in order for, so that I can get out there and help.' She shook her head, her knuckles flashing white. 'People who are truly powerless on their own, and I have no right to say such things about my own experiences.'

'You have every right.'

Because she'd clearly been punishing herself with those same words for heaven knew how long. Since she'd married into royalty or long before then too.

'Now you're just humouring me to be kind.' She gave him another of her shy smiles. A hundred times genuine. He'd bet his life on it.

'I've been called many things in my life, but *kind* isn't one that springs to mind.'

Fierce or *fun*. Depending on the circumstance. *Stubborn* or *obstinate* to use his father's most recent favourite when his retirement had been forced upon him. But, *kind*?

'I don't believe you.' She rested her head against the back of the sofa, not so shy now as her gaze narrowed on him. 'Your eyes are kind.'

'Regardless of what you think of my eyes...' Though her words did warm his voice, his smile '... I always say what I mean, Cassie. As for what you are going through as a person, not as an ex-princess or as a lady of the English aristocracy, but as a person with real feelings, it's a lot under any normal circumstances. Divorce is one of the hardest, most stressful challenges anyone can face...'

'You sound like you're talking from experience.'

'No, not me personally. Though there were times as a kid that I thought maybe my parents would have been better off apart. And even then, the arguments were mainly about Dad not being home enough, so maybe not.' He gave a smile that was so caught up in her present hurt he wasn't sure if it came across as more of a grimace. 'But what I'm trying to say is, at least most of us get to go about our business without the whole world breathing down our necks through a camera lens and forming an ill-informed opinion on it. It stands to reason you're going to have your moments.'

She gave a soft huff. 'I've not been permitted such moments for a long time.'

'And how do you cope with that?'

'I'm not sure I am coping all that well.'

'I don't know, from where I'm sitting you seem to have done remarkably well.'

'What?' She gave a brittle laugh, and he missed the woman of seconds before—the one that thought him kind and looked increasingly relaxed in his presence. 'By spilling my heart out to a total stranger who I met only yesterday?'

'You carry yourself with such grace and poise, I never would have known that the woman who stood before me last night and thought to offer out her jacket was the same woman being hounded by the press, vilified by a royal family, and as you've now explained, ostracised by her own. You are a wonder, Cassie. And if you don't know it, allow me to tell you it is so.'

Her mouth twitched, the warmth once again blooming in her cheeks and her chest and, *Dieu*, was he glad to see it. 'Ah, well, last night you had me distracted.'

He fought the reciprocal warmth in his chest, the cheeky twitch to his own mouth. 'And when you're out in public, I assume you have a team with you to help keep the masses at bay?'

She gave another laugh, this time it sounded more delirious than brittle and it had him worried. Not that he could say why.

'I don't go out.'

'What do you mean, you don't go out?'

'Just what I said.'

'Cassie, everyone goes out at some point.'

'Not me.'

She couldn't be serious. Something inside his chest shrivelled.

'So last night…before you came upon me?'

'I'd been to the rooftop bar for a drink.'

'Alone?'

She nodded.

'Beni is a sweetheart and is kind enough to open it after everyone else has gone to bed.'

'Because that way you don't have to see anyone?'

Again, she nodded, and again he felt this weird shrivelling sensation inside his chest. If he wasn't so traumatised by the whole conversation, he'd be touched that she had taken the time to learn the name of his bar staff.

'Don't get me wrong, sometimes there's the odd person, but in the main, it's just me.'

She smiled. Actually *smiled*. And he wanted to cry. Which was as ridiculous as this whole situation. Ridiculously unfair.

'When you've lived enough days and nights being chased down, Hugo, with no regard for your personal space, you begin to crave those quiet hours while the city sleeps. And the witching hour has kind of become my time to dine. Though I don't really eat as such, more get some fresh air while everyone else is asleep.'

He took up his coffee, needing something to do that wasn't taking her hand and walking her out of here right now…

'How long have you been here for, Cassie?'

'What? Staying at Louis's?'

'Oui.'

'A month.'

'And for that entire time, you haven't left this apartment?'

She gave a subtle shake of her head, as though she could sense the storm brewing within him as he stifled a curse with a sip of his coffee. 'Have you seen the sights, walked the river, been to the Louvre, the parks?'

She was shaking her head at everything, and he was—he was losing his mind at the very idea that she could have been in the city for a whole month and seen nothing. Nothing at all!

'But I am lucky because your hotel is well positioned. I have a view of the Eiffel Tower, Arc de Triomphe and Champs-Élysées depending on where I stand. The balcony is vast, the private plunge pool a delight, and the room service is all-encompassing.'

'But, Cassie!' Her eyes flared and he immediately softened his posture and his words— remembering that for all she was fierce in some ways, she was still that skittish kitten in others, and he couldn't blame her. Living a life being papped 24-7. A life like Sara had led. 'Living inside these four walls day in, day out, is not living.'

'People regularly survive on a whole lot less.'

'Survive, sure. One's sanity, however…?'

'And as we have established, I cannot move for reporters…some days I only have to turn my head in the wrong direction in the presence of the wrong person and someone will make something of it, and that could be as catastrophic as a natural disaster on the world's stage.'

As he had seen for himself. But to know that she had escaped one form of prison only to land herself in another—his Parisian paradise of all places—when she had the City of Love on her doorstep.

To live in it like a prisoner, when her only crime had been marriage to a prince.

A prince whose own reputation was scandalous at best, who'd managed to make her feel ridiculed and laughed at in her own home. *Mon Dieu*, if he ever met the man…

'Do you care what the world thinks that much?'

'It's not a question of care as it is being impossible to ignore. They're like pack animals and I'm their prey. I can't go about my day without being set upon. Though that's probably being unfair to pack animals…'

'But now you're divorced, surely, things will start to ease?'

'When the Duponts stop stirring the pot, perhaps they will. Right now, they need me to lose face so that he may save his. It is far safer for me to keep a low profile while our divorce is so fresh. He needs to find a new bride, someone willing to look past his reputation like I once did, and they will paint the picture they need in order to make the future look how they wish.'

'No matter what damage it does to you?'

'The picture is not yet tainted enough.'

He cursed. The heartless nature of it all too much to take.

'Precisely. And I have my own dreams to consider and protect.' Eyes likes emeralds, glittering and bright, drifted to the drawings she'd set aside. 'While all those girls dreamt of being a princess, I dreamt of one day having my own fashion label.'

He'd warrant she'd dreamt of a lot more than that…before her prince had shattered those dreams, had she wanted mini princes and mini princesses to fill her fairy-tale castle?

And why on earth had his head gone there? Maybe because he could see her as a mother?

With the good heart she wore on her sleeve…
it must have driven the Prince crazy that she
bore that trait so effortlessly, that people
flocked to it, trusted it.

'I even had a name…'

He lifted his chin, focused on what she was
saying and not the wild assumptions he was
making about the man he really would like to
put in a ring and go ten rounds with.

'Care to share?'

'Cassie Couture.' She laughed softly. 'I
know. I know. It's probably a little cheesy.'

'Only as cheesy as Chevalier Clubs, perhaps.'

They shared a laugh. 'How true.'

'And if it's good enough for Coco Chanel…'

'Ah, life goals!' Her gaze lifted to his. 'As
for the dream itself, it still feels out of reach,
like the foolish dreams of a foolish child. But
maybe, one day…'

'And the drawings?'

'Louis thinks he could test some out on the
catwalk next February.'

'Louis? Why not you? Surely with your
name, you could secure funding, put yourself out there?'

She nibbled on her lip. 'For now, I'm con-
tent hiding out up here, sketching.'

'And letting someone else take the credit?'

'All big names have a team behind them, and we all have to start somewhere. I'm lucky I have someone like Louis willing to take a chance on me.' She was saying the right things, even if they sounded hollow to him. 'Hopefully, soon enough, the press furore will calm, and I'll be able to step outside once more, live my life again.'

'How I wish you were talking metaphorically, but you're not.'

'No.'

'But that's not healthy, can't you see? What about fresh air? What about everyday things like taking a walk, fetching some groceries, seeing a film, eating out?'

Mon Dieu, the list was endless. His father's firm—*his* now—provided protection for people like her day in, day out for this precise reason. To make sure they lived as normal a life as possible. To make life about saying 'yes' again, within reason. So long as situations were assessed, prepared for, managed.

She smiled. 'You know what I miss most?'

'No.' But he knew it was going to kill him, whatever it was.

'Aside from the charity work, which I truly

am desperate to get back to, but I don't want it tainted by all this noise.'

'I think you put too much stock in what the Duponts are throwing about. Your charities will still benefit from your presence regardless.'

'I want the attention to be *on* the charity work. While it's on my personal life, it defeats that.'

He nodded. 'I take your point…so you were saying?'

'You'll think I'm odd.'

'Try me.'

She beamed. 'Running.'

'Running?' He choked over his coffee. Not what he'd expected her to say. Enjoying a drink in a bar uninterrupted. Taking her art to the park. Sketching in a museum or a fashion house where she could feel inspired. Even dress shopping. But *running*?

'Yes. See. I told you.'

'Of all the things…'

She raised her brows, eyes sparking. 'You thought I was going to say clothes shopping, didn't you?'

'In my defence, you'd already said charity work, so…'

He shifted against the fabric of the sofa,

willing it to open up and swallow him whole. He'd never considered himself sexist before.

'I apologise.' And swiftly, he went back to the reason he'd landed himself in this mess, 'So, you like to run?'

'I do. And I used to like to run outdoors, even back in Sérignone. The palace grounds were vast enough that I could fit in a five-k run without ever having to venture outside the gates…that was until the rumours became too much for the palace.'

'The rumours?'

'Oh, yes.' She gave a wry smile. 'At which point the King put a stop to my exercise outdoors.'

Hugo clenched his jaw to stifle a curse.

'Apparently a princess in running gear, exerting herself no less, is unacceptable. I was seen as flaunting myself in front of the grounds staff, courting trouble.'

'Meanwhile his son could carry on how he liked?'

'He knew I would listen.'

He clenched his jaw once more and there went a tooth, Hugo was sure of it.

She didn't wait for him to respond, which was lucky, because there were no words Hugo could give that he would deem fit for her ears as her gaze drifted to the French windows. The balcony with its abundance of flowers hanging on to the end of the season, just a sample of what she'd see if she was to hit the vast and varied parks Paris had to offer, not to mention the incredible views along the river Seine.

So much beauty on her doorstep, it was a crime she didn't get to see it. Had she *ever* seen the Seine up close? He didn't dare ask. She'd probably tell him another horror story. And he didn't think his teeth could take any more grinding.

Whether it was the similarity to Sara, the knowledge of what Cassie had been through, what she was *still* going through at the hands of the Duponts and the press…

'But yes, I love to run. I love to feel the wind against my face, in my hair…it didn't matter what troubles I faced, there was something about the way I could lose myself in the rhythmic rush of it that just worked. Some women choose yoga—' she shrugged '—I choose to run.'

'Then do it.'

Because in that moment, he was one hundred percent determined to see her do it. And as soon as humanly possible.

Her head snapped around, her eyes flaring wide as she looked at him like he was crazy to suggest it. And maybe he was.

'Just like that…get into my kit, my trainers and poof, out the door?'

'It's what millions do every day.'

'Have you been listening to me? I'd barely make it into the hotel lobby without a wall of people forming a human assault course. I'd do myself an injury, if not someone else.'

'What about your witching hour?'

Her eyes flared further, which he wouldn't have believed possible. But then, she really did have the biggest, greenest, most alluring…

'Because that's going to be so safe?'

'You'd be safe with me.'

She gawped at him, a solitary strand of glossy brown hair sticking to her luscious pink lips. 'You can't be serious?'

'Absolutely. And if you don't want to use your security detail, I will bring in—' She pulled a face that gave him pause. 'What's that look about?'

She hesitated.

'Cassie?'

'I don't have a detail.'

'You don't…'

'Do you see any guards hovering, Mr Chevalier?'

No, he hadn't noticed any extra security people hanging about, but then the best always managed to blend into the background. And as she had already said, she didn't venture outside of her room, so it wasn't like she went anywhere to require one. But someone of Cassie's status would have at least one Certified Protection Officer on a permanent basis.

'Obviously, not right now, while we're here, but if we were to venture out…'

'If we were to venture out, I wouldn't suddenly have the funds to pay for one. And yes, before you say it, I am aware of the risks. My continued love-hate relationship with the world, the would-be stalkers and so on. However, I took nothing from Georges in the divorce. We have no children to provide for and so it didn't feel right. And yes, I am more than aware of how foolish many consider that to be, my lawyer was very open on the matter, but I just wanted to be free of the Duponts and any hold they had over me. Yes, that has kind of backfired in the aftermath, but in the long term karma will hopefully be my payback.

'As for my parents, they have to all intents and purposes disowned me, and until I can sell my designs, I am beholden to my friends and your hotel's excellent hospitality and exceptional security. So, I will make do. Can we consider this conversation done?'

Why did Hugo feel like this conversation had been done many times before him? With her lawyer, like she had already said, and Louis too, perhaps.

'We absolutely can.'

'Bon.' And then she smiled as she considered him with a tilt of her head. 'You would really take me running?'

'Are you saying I don't look like the type to run?' He feigned insult over his physical ability rather than accept she was questioning the generosity of the offer. Because then he'd have to question it himself. And that would mean examining his own good conscience and whether he was in his right mind to suggest it too. After everything that had happened with Sara—gone *wrong* with Sara— But this was about getting things right this time… With access to his father's firm— *his* firm now, he could make sure they were well protected, and he could give her the freedom she so desperately deserved and needed.

'Because I can assure you, Cassie, I'm quite capable of a five-k run at a decent pace. And further if you really wanted to push it out, but any longer and you'll be hitting the early-morning commuters and I believe that defeats the point.'

'It's not your ability to go the distance that I'm questioning, it's the fact you're offering to run at that ungodly hour.'

He shrugged. 'If we stick to the Seine, it's lit and, aside from the odd stretch of cobbles, perfectly safe.'

'You really are serious…'

'You're awake anyway, so why not?'

'But you're not! Unless you're planning another…'

She coloured, clearly thinking of his naked night-time misadventures.

'I don't plan them. They happen when they happen.'

'Of course, I shouldn't have teased. Forgive me.'

'There's nothing to forgive.' And this time he softened his tone, stripping it of the defensive note she'd clearly picked up on, because it wasn't directed at her. She wasn't the reason he'd been wandering the corridors in such a state.

'They must be quite unsettling for you…to go to sleep in one place and wake up in another.'

'Thankfully they don't happen all that often. It's usually when I'm not sleeping very well to begin with.'

Her brows twitched but she didn't press. Was it a learned response to life in the royal family, her time before with her parents or was she leaving it up to him? Whichever the case, he found himself starting to explain…

'I've only just returned from LA which means I'm still on their time.'

'LA? Business or pleasure?'

He gave a tight laugh. 'Family. Which sort of makes it a hashed attempt at both with a side order of stress.'

'Ah…' She placed her mug down on the coffee table, pulled the sleeves of her jumper over her hands and curled back into the sofa. 'Goes without saying that you have a friendly ear willing to listen if you want to offload some of that?'

He choked on another laugh, because in that moment he realised two things: one, he'd never spoken to anyone about the pressure he was now under, running his hotel empire alongside his father's global security company.

Made worse by his father's inability to let the latter go.

And two, he was about to spill it all to Cassie. Not the caricature the press liked to flaunt. Poised, shy, scandalous or otherwise. But the very real, very warm, very attractive brunette, curled up on the sofa beside him. Patiently waiting for him to speak as though she had all the time in the world for it. For him.

And it felt like bliss.

A sensation he'd never quite experienced before... The world and his wife could wait...or rather, the global companies on his shoulders could. And as though summoned, his phone began to ring, and he checked the screen.

It was Eduardo. CEO of Dad's—*his*—security firm.

Eduardo was capable. He'd been his father's number two for twenty years. He could cope for a day. A *Satur*day. He should just ignore it, follow her lead and hide out from the noise.

'Do you need to get that?' she asked.

Did he? He was a few months into his reign. Would it do for Eduardo to report back to Dad—which he would do at some point—that he was deflecting calls?

But you're the boss.

Still, he needed Dad to back off, which he

wasn't going to do if he thought Hugo wasn't getting the job done. 'Give me two minutes.'

'So, LA?' Cassie said as he returned to her, his phone tucked away, his smile enigmatic. 'Yes.'

She imagined him, the broad-shouldered man before her with his kind blue eyes and chiselled features, as a son. With a doting mother and a proud father. She could see it so readily. The warm and happy picture painting itself. Could see them all walking down the palm-lined strip of Sunset Boulevard or Rodeo Drive, places she too had been. But she believed her experience to have been so very different.

'My parents—or rather, my mother has decided they should retire out there.'

'Sounds lovely.'

'My mother thinks so.'

'You don't?'

'Oh, I do.'

She frowned. 'So, it's your father who doesn't?'

'My father thinks any home that's not on the same continent as the company headquarters he has been forced to leave behind is anything but lovely.'

'I take it the company headquarters are here?'

'Oui.'

'And he likes to keep a toe in?'

'A toe?' He chuckled, the sound deep and throaty as it rippled through his burly frame and did something unidentifiable to her own. Something that felt awfully close to excitement. 'He likes to keep his whole body in.'

'Was he not ready to retire?'

He eased back into the sofa, one arm along its back, one leg hooked over the other by the ankle, everything about him relaxed, though she sensed that, like a panther, he was never far from pouncing should the need arise. She knew he had the physique for it, beneath the crisp dark shirt, the carefully pressed chinos too.

'If I'm brutally honest, I think my mother feared we'd be carrying him out of his company in a box. At first it was getting him out of the field, then it was getting him to simply stop.'

She frowned. 'The field? You make the hospitality industry sound like the military.'

He gave another chuckle. 'Oh, we're not in the same business. Well, we weren't. We are now. Or at least I am.' He paused. Took a breath. 'I'm not making much sense, am I?'

She smiled. 'Perhaps it's your turn to start at the beginning.'

'You're right, I should.' He returned her smile, though it lacked the warmth that had existed moments ago, and she wondered at its cause. Was it his father? The business? Businesses, if they weren't one and the same. And the recent stress he'd eluded too? 'My father's company, now mine since he retired, is in the business of protection—money, data, people—if there's a risk, we protect it.'

'So, you're in leisure *and* protection… How come you ventured into one when your father was in the other?'

'I guess you could say, I carved out my own path.'

There was something about the way he said it. Something that made her want to delve deeper, like a child wanting to ask 'why?' on repeat. And perhaps she would have if he hadn't said, 'but he always intended for me to take on his firm one day, when he felt I was ready.'

'And how old is your father?'

'He celebrated his seventy-fifth birthday while I was in LA.'

'Seventy-fifth!'

'Quite. And I say *celebrated* in the loosest sense of the term. The man does not take kindly to growing old.'

'But growing old is a privilege.'

'Of that he would agree, he just doesn't appreciate the ailments that come with it.'

'Or the retirement?' Because to wait until one was seventy-five to hand over the reins...?

'Or the son who has filled his shoes.'

She stilled, caught off guard by the unexpected bitterness in the man who, up until now, had been the biggest, strongest, cuddliest, and sexiest of teddy bears if such a thing were to exist. 'I'm sure that's not true.'

He fell silent, his gaze shifting to the outdoors as she lost him to his thoughts. Maybe she'd been too quick to paint Hugo's family as picture-perfect. But it was a habit she'd formed long ago. Imagining what everyone else's life was like to avoid having to think about her own.

'I don't know, it's complicated for him.' He gave an awkward shrug. 'To see his son grow stronger as he gets weaker. Especially when things were so much harder for him. Hell, at my age he was fleeing Poland with nothing more than the clothes on his back...' His mouth twisted to the side as he stroked the stubble of his chin, admiration flashing in his eyes. 'And that's another secret I probably shouldn't share, especially when it isn't mine to give…'

'I think we've already established that secrets are safe here.'

She tucked a hand around her legs as his gaze returned to her. Gave him a smile that she hoped would encourage him because she had shared so much of herself, and she hoped he felt secure enough to share a little of himself too. He returned her smile and for a moment, they shared nothing but that look, though she felt it—the connection, the warmth of it. It caught at the air, at her breath, at her pulse…

'My father was part of the Służba Bezpieczeństwa—the SB, Poland's secret police,' he added at her raised brow. 'He didn't agree with Soviet rule, wanted out and he came to Paris. Went into security. It suited his natural talents. He met Mum. Fell in love. They got married. He took her name. And the rest as they say, is history. He built a home and a global security firm that protects everything from data to individuals. He left Poland with nothing. No family, no support. And I guess, I grew up with all of that…'

She frowned. 'But why would that make it hard for him to hand the business over to you now? Surely he can't begrudge what he gave you.'

It didn't make any sense to her. The man should surely be proud that he had provided for his family and their future. Escaped a life that he hadn't wanted for himself or for his future family. And to see his son take on the mantle of his firm…

'I think it's more that his life made him hard, whereas he perceives me as the opposite.'

'I still don't follow.'

A shadow chased over his face. A shadow she wanted to catch and probe and soothe away. But before she could press, he shifted forward. Gave an awkward laugh. Changing the mood up so entirely she didn't feel she could.

'I'm not sure I do either. I'm rambling.'

'I don't think you are. I'm just trying to piece it together.'

'How did we get to this point again?'

He gave her a lopsided grin that made her

stomach flip over. Almost making her forget the sombre mood of seconds before.

'I think you were telling me how you ended up responsible for two global companies in two very different industries.'

'Ah, yes. And I went off on a tangent telling you all about how my father doesn't want to give up what he built, despite building me to give it to...'

'That's quite the conundrum.'

'It is, and so when I went to LA last week, I gifted him a digi-detox for his birthday in the hope that it would gift me some temporary quiet in return.'

She laughed. 'You did *what*?'

'It's one of my most exclusive resorts— a Caribbean haven, cut off from the outside world. No comms, only paradise. A true digital detox for a month. No expense spared. They should have checked in yesterday.'

'And your father was happy to receive such a gift?'

'I'm not sure *happy* was the word I would use, but desperate times call for desperate measures. He needs to find a new way of living, and I'm hoping a month on the island with a life coach and other specialists in their fields will help retrain his brain. And my mother will get a holiday.'

'Is he really that bad?'

'Put it this way, in the three months my father has been retired, he has called me almost daily for an update. Between him and his number two—now my number two, Eduardo, the man who just called—I'm on speed dial. I figured at least this way he's forced to try a new way of living and Mum gets to relax.'

'And you get some peace.'

'One can hope.'

'And no more sleepwalking.'

'That's the dream,' he teased.

'What about Eduardo? What does he make of your father's constant check-ins?'

'Eduardo could run the company with his eyes closed. He knows what he's doing, my father just never left him alone enough.'

'And yet, he is the one ringing you on a Saturday?'

'More out of habit than necessity.'

'I see. And is that a habit you intend to break.'

He paused. 'Perhaps. Right now, my priority is exerting my authority. For forty years my father was the boss. Now I am, and it's

important that they know that. My father in-
cluded.'

She heard the vehemence in that one statement. The fierce sense of ownership. Whether
he was trying to prove it to himself or his non-
present father or employees, it spoke volumes.

'And you will. And you will do him proud
too.'

He gave a grunt.

'But you need to be your own man in the
process. Don't lose yourself in trying to become him. You need to do it your own way.'

She didn't know where the words came
from, or why it felt so important that she said
them. Perhaps it was the sense that he was
battling a vision of the man his father wanted
him to be, rather than simply being the man
he was...and she knew how that felt. How it
felt to be caged by someone else's ideal.

His clear blue eyes narrowed on her. 'You
know, for a morning coffee, this got deep
pretty quickly.'

'And there was I, thinking we couldn't get
much closer than last night's escapade.'

'You're not going to let me forget that, are
you?'

She gave him a smile full of the warmth
she felt inside. 'It will be nice to get to know

you well enough to let you forget, Hugo.' Because she wanted to get to know him better. She wanted to make a friend. A true friend. Not one that was looking for a way into Princess Cassandra's inner circle. But one that she could confide in and who could talk to her in return. 'If you will come for coffee again?'

'I'd like that, Cassie. Very much.'

CHAPTER FOUR

THE NEXT MORNING Hugo was eating his breakfast while reviewing the financial headlines when his phone started to ring. He checked the ID. Mickie. On a Sunday. This early?

His friend rarely saw 8:00 a.m. on a weekday, let alone on a Sunday.

What kind of mischief had his friend got into now?

He swiped the call to answer and prepared himself for the worst. Of course, there was nothing to say Mickie wasn't on the other side of the globe in which case it would be late rather than early for him. And that probably made the potential trouble worse…

'Hugo, my friend, you got something you want to tell me?'

'I don't know that I do, since you're the one calling me?'

Mickie's laugh rumbled down the phone. 'So that's how you're going to play it?'

'Play what?' Hugo put down the toast he was about to bite into. 'It's too early for riddles, Mickie.'

'Come on, don't be coy! Fancy my surprise this morning when I wake up to see you plastered all over the celebrity gossip channels.'

'The *what*?'

'Funny, you sound about as shocked as I was.'

'Is this some joke?' Hugo pressed his forehead into his palm and took a breath. It really was too early for this.

'Skylar, chuck us that remote…' his friend said.

'Skylar?' Hugo repeated. 'Who's…?'

'My date from last night. You didn't think I was the one catching up with the celeb goss, did you?'

Hugo didn't know what to think. Didn't *want* to think for fear of what was happening outside his four walls if Mickie knew all about it and thought it was worthy of this kind of a call.

'Thank you, darl.'

'For what?' Hugo said.

'I wasn't talking to you.'

Clearly, but…

'Get yourself onto Celeb 101, Hugo. Your mug's right there, right now.'

'Celeb 101?'

'Use the TV guide…you'll have it there somewhere. Right next to those 24-7 reality TV channels…'

Like Hugo would know where any of those were either…but on autopilot, he switched on the TV embedded in the wall above his sleek black countertop. Searched the guide with rising trepidation. Especially as his phone started to chime with another incoming call, then another. He eyed the screen. One was Eduardo, another was his PA.

This wasn't good. His skin started to crawl, the hairs on his neck rising. There was only one reason he could have made that kind of news…one reason only…

'You found it yet?'

Just. He clicked on the channel and the screen filled with a pimped-up news studio starring living, breathing Ken and Barbie lookalikes seated behind a desk. A fuchsia-pink ticker tape ran along the bottom spewing out 'news'. And there, in the top right corner of the screen were photos. Photos of *them*. Cassie and Hugo. Him on her doorstep with the flowers. Her with her naked shoulder, all flushed and—*for the love of…*

'In the two years since her separation from

Prince Georges,' the Barbie lookalike was saying, 'speculation has mounted over the breakdown of what was once considered the marriage of the decade if not the century. A real life fairy tale has become a tale of tragedy. People were quick to blame it on the Playboy Prince, his reputation making him an easy target, but with stories surrounding the Princess, friends and ex-lovers selling stories to the tabloids, and now this latest scandal, it really does beg the question, do we truly know who this woman is? We were so quick to adore her, yet here she is jumping from the bed of one man to another, the seal on her divorce barely dry. And who is this man? Our very own Suzie is out in the field to tell us more…'

'Got to hand it to you, man, I didn't know you had it in you.'

He'd forgotten Mickie was on the line. He'd forgotten the world existed. He'd forgotten everything but the woman next door and the impact such a report was going to have on her.

Such a ridiculous report, but a report out in the world all the same. And one with a picture to back it up. A picture he might as well as have handed to the greedy mob pounding the pavement outside…

Taken inside *his* hotel, on *his* watch, on *his* floor.

'*Merde!*'

Cassie hadn't slept. Not properly. She kept tossing and turning, feeling the after-effects of Hugo's presence well into the night. The apartment had never felt so vast and so empty… even with Louis's abundance of ornamental delights.

She'd become accustomed to her own company long ago. Being in her own company amongst others most of all. Loneliness was something she'd learnt to live with rather than bemoan. And normally she would throw her restlessness into her designs or lose herself in the pages of a good book. Always something creative if she could choose.

But she'd been left with this frenetic energy that she just couldn't shift, so here she was on the treadmill, trying her second run of the morning because all else had failed. She increased her speed because a jog wasn't working. Turned the volume on her music up too.

A sprint to Taylor Swift full blast—this *had* to work, surely?

She snatched up her towel from the rail on the treadmill to swipe away the layer of perspiration already thick across her skin. Adjusted her earbuds. Slugged her water. And felt Swift's lyrics to her core as she pounded the rolling road beneath her feet.

For years she'd worked hard to be the woman her family had wanted her to be, eager to please them, eager for a kind word too. Then it had been all about the Prince and *his* family. Trading one impossible mission for another.

She hadn't stopped to think about her own happiness in any of it. She'd been too focused on their happiness equating to her own. Now she'd finally broken free. Finally realised the only person she could truly depend on for her own happiness was herself. And to achieve it, she needed to find herself. Who she was without the noise of the outside world and the constraints she'd lived her life bound by thus far. And she was getting there. Kind of.

So why did she feel all at sea again?

She had no clue and she wasn't hopping off this treadmill until the noise in her brain resembled something more like the quiet she had found of late. The quiet of—

The ring of the apartment's ancient doorbell broke through Swift's triumphant chorus, and she checked the time. Frowned. It was still early. Not that the time made any difference to her surprise. She wasn't expecting anyone.

Room service had already been and gone with her breakfast plates. That day's house-keeping too. It came again, more insistent. She hadn't imagined it.

She hit the pause button and grabbed her towel, headed to the door.

It couldn't be Hugo. It had been a day. Twenty-four hours since their impromptu coffee date. Her eyes caught on the flowers he had brought her, the classic white bouquet bloom-ing bright and beautiful in the hallway. He had no reason to call again so soon. Unless—she smiled helplessly into her towel—he too had found himself in some curious state of limbo since he'd vacated her orbit. How weird that would be.

Weird and kind of wonderful if she was being totally honest with herself.

Careful, Cassie, don't be getting carried away.

Especially over a man like Hugo, who would be so easy to get carried away by…

She was supposed to be focusing on herself and what she wanted from life.

But what if that something was a six-foot-four hunk of male charm?

And that was precisely the kind of want that would land her in trouble. The kind of trouble her ex and the rest of the royal family would use to their advantage and she would do well to avoid. Though who was to say he was interested in her in the same way? She hardly had the best track record when it came to reading others. Case in point!

Love, affection, desire…what did she truly know of it? A bit fat zero.

Hugo had been kind and understanding, that was all, and now she was likely projecting her own feelings onto him. Just as she had done with Georges in those early days.

She caught her reflection in the free-standing gilt-edged mirror at the end of the hall and grimaced. Both at her thoughts and at her flushed state of disarray. Hardly presentable. Unless one was trying out for a sports advertisement, and even then she'd leave a lot to be desired. She lacked the glow of sun exposure for a start.

And here she was, debating her appearance like it was him on the other side of the door, projecting her hopes, when it was probably—

The doorbell rang again, and this time Hugo's urgent cry came with it, 'Cassie!'

Okay, so it *was* him, but his voice…

With a sharp frown, she swiftly unbolted the door and yanked it wide. 'Hugo, what's wrong?'

'Cassie, Dieu merci!'

He grabbed her arms and she stiffened, heat surging to her already scorched core. Tiny, frenzied currents, the likes of which she'd never felt before and barely understood now, zipping through her and spreading fast.

She gawped up at him and he cursed, his hands falling away as he stepped back to give her space.

'Désolé. I shouldn't have.'

She closed her mouth, swallowed. What was going on within her? Desire? Is that what this was? The heat, the fire, the need…because Georges had never done this to her. Not with a simple grasp of his hands.

'You *are* okay?' His desperate gaze raked over her. 'Aren't you?'

Answer him…

She nodded, her unease building by the second. Because the words coming out of his mouth suggested something was wrong. Very wrong. And it was pressing back the heat his contact had stirred up, common sense overriding her body as she forced the words through her teeth, 'What's wrong?'

'You don't know?' He dragged a hand down his face. 'You haven't seen the news? How can you—can I come in?'

'So many questions, Hugo.' She gave a shaky laugh, clutched her towel beneath her chin as goose-bumps prickled across her skin. Aware more than ever that she was wearing nothing more than an exercise bra and cropped shorts.

'And I'm not the only one with questions, believe me.'

A trickle ran down her spine, the chill on the rise as she dabbed at her cheeks, which felt fuzzy and faint. 'You're scaring me.'

'I know and I'm sorry, Cassie. But it's best we talk inside.'

She backed up, making enough space for him to enter as he swung the door closed on them both. Though she didn't move from the vestibule. Her stomach rolling too much to put one foot in front of the other.

'What is it?' she said to his back as he made his way into the living area, scanning the room like one would for danger, checking every nook, every cranny.

'Hugo?'

'I thought you would have seen. I thought you weren't answering because you *had* seen, and you were—I don't know. Despairing. Panicking. Packing!'

He rubbed the back of his head, up and down, eyes chasing over the objects in the room, anywhere but her, and slowly she joined him.

'How could you not have heard the commotion out there?'

He threw a hand towards the balcony and the muted sounds beyond. Granted, there was more noise coming from the street than usual. But she'd long ago stopped listening to what happened outside the four walls she was in. Beyond the conversation she was involved in too. The whispered words of judgement, the gossip, and the snide remarks.

'Hugo,' she said softly, wishing to steady him, because she sensed that whatever this was, it had more to do with her than it did him. And she was used to her own baggage, he didn't need to carry it for her. 'Whatever it is, I am sure it can't be as bad as—'

'Someone saw me come to your room yesterday morning,' he said as he paced up and down. 'They took a photograph and it's everywhere. *We're* everywhere.'

Cassie's heart did a weird little dance, rising part-way up her throat. 'What do you mean, *we're* everywhere?'

Though she knew, of course she knew. She'd been the subject of enough tittle-tattle over the years to know exactly what he meant. But she was stalling. Biding her time while she processed it.

'I'm sorry, Cassie.'

He stilled, his eyes finding hers. She saw the guilt weighing heavy in his crystal-clear blue eyes. Saw the guilt as she also imagined the glee in her ex-husband's face.

'The world thinks we're together. That you and I—' He shook his head. 'I'm sorry. I don't know how this could have happened, and had I known the trouble I would cause you by coming to your room with flowers and—and the kind of headlines it would stir up...'

Slowly she brought her hand back to her chest, steadied herself against the onslaught of what was to come—what was already happening out there. The Duponts wouldn't hang around. They'd be straight on this salacious piece of ammo, using it to elevate Georges's reputation and sully hers.

And all because she'd had the gall to get up and walk away.

'I don't understand how you didn't know.'

Hugo snapped her back into the present, his face blazing with concern and obliterating Georges from her mind.

'My phone is always on Do Not Disturb,' she said, her voice devoid of emotion. Because this wasn't Hugo's fault. This wasn't hers. And this *would* blow over. It was the nature of the beast. She just had to keep it in perspective. 'I don't watch live TV. I don't listen to the radio. Only the people that I care about and want to hear from get through, the rest I mute.'

'But out there, the noise…' He gestured towards the balcony once more…at the commotion outside that suggested there were more vehicles. More press. More people. The hotel would be cursing her name. *He* would be cursing her name. 'I'm sorry, I will sort myself somewhere else to stay as soon as possible. This is the last thing you and your guests need.'

'Oh, no, you won't. You're fine to stay here.'

'But Hugo…'

'I mean it, Cassie. Louis gifted you his home, and I stand by that offer.'

The stubborn set to his jaw, the flash of steel in his blue eyes told her he meant it. 'I'm sorry.'

'You don't need to apologise to me.'

'Oh, I do. Because if they're making something out of this, I'm sure you're not coming off too lightly either. If not in today's news reports, then tomorrow's. Georges and his ego will see to it.'

'I couldn't care less about myself in all of this. It's you I'm worried about. You must have a PR team, a spokesperson you can liaise with to issue a formal response?'

She gave a soft huff. 'A PR team? Because they don't cost the earth.'

'Right. Of course you don't. We can use mine.'

'No, Hugo. There's no point. They'll print what they want to print. You deny it and they'll think there's more to it. And what are you going to say? Tell them the truth of how we met and tackle *that* tale, too? No. It will blow over. They'll tire of it eventually.'

'And in the meantime, what? You sit back and let them rip apart your character?'

He was so fierce. So ready to fight for her honour. And there was something magical and wonderful and surreal about it. No one had ever looked ready to do battle for her. Not ever.

'Sticks and stones, Hugo.'

'No, Cassie.' He shook his head, legs wide, fists on hips. Fighting stance. 'This happened on my watch, in my hotel. I besmirched your character and I need to fix it.'

'This wasn't your fault.'

He raised his hand. 'It doesn't matter that it wasn't my intent. What's done is done and I will not stand by and have them twist the person you are into someone you are not. You don't deserve it.'

Her heart swooned. *Positively* swooned. 'Then what do you suggest?'

'For starters, I'll be speaking to the head of security. It must have been one of the cleaners from the lift. You can't access this floor without the right pass and there was only me, you, and the staff that morning.'

She shook her head. 'I don't want to cause any more trouble, Hugo. My presence has already caused enough. All the extra security, the extra checks, the chaos outside the doors… I'm a headache for everyone concerned.'

'But what they did was wrong—it needs to be investigated and the person responsible held accountable.'

'I'd rather just let it blow over.'

'That out there isn't blowing over any time

soon, and in the meantime, what? You're going to hide away even more?'

'If I have to.'

'No, Cassie. You've lived your entire life on hold for others. It's time you started living it for you, and you have the city of Paris on your doorstep to get outside and enjoy.'

She gave a shaky laugh. 'No one could enjoy Paris hounded by that lot.'

'I think it's high time you tried another strategy.'

Her chin lifted, ears and heart pricking with something akin to hope. 'Like what?'

'I think you should give them more not less.'

'What on earth are you talking about?'

'They think you and I are together so let them think that. Let them think that rather than a fling, a brazen hop from one man's bed to another, that this is more than that. Deeper than that. A romantic tryst in the world's most romantic of cities. And while we give them more, I can give you what you deserve. I can give you Paris. I can show you the delights of the city, get you out of these four walls and out into the real world. Let me make up for my part in what has happened and give you something you're long overdue in return.'

'I told you…' She gave a laugh that sounded as deranged as she suddenly felt, because his idea was making her feel all manner of things. Some crazy. Some fabulous. Some wonderfully thrilling. 'It isn't possible. I can't step foot out of this building without a gaggle of reporters and photographers dogging my every step, without drawing the attention of every innocent passer-by too and causing chaos. It isn't pleasant for anyone.'

'And so you've hidden yourself away. But by hiding your face, you've made it a rarity. Don't you see?'

'What choice do I have?'

'You can choose to give them more not less. And soon your face will be a novelty no more. And that rare photo opportunity will be as common as the next among a million of snaps. Granted, they won't all be of your best side, but if you can learn to live with the odd stray bit of snot or lucky bird poo drop…?'

'Hugo…' She shook her head, laughing at the ridiculousness of it all. Because it was ridiculous—*wasn't* it?

'Think about it, Cassie. It's all about supply and demand, give them more and they will demand less. And in the meantime, you get out of these four walls and live in the real world.'

'And the stories they are spreading, what about those?'

'By hiding away you've allowed the rumours to build, fed the gossip and the whispers, let them draw their own conclusions. Why not paint the tale you'd rather have spread? A love story, however short-lived, is far better than the harlot they seem determined to label you as.'

'Not them,' she said through her teeth.

'What was that?'

'I said, not them. Georges and his family. They're the ones who want to paint me as such. I told you—it suits them to make me look bad. He needs a new wife and quickly, with his father...'

She bit her lip. She'd said too much. She may not have any affection for the Duponts, but there were things she was not permitted to divulge. The King's health and her ex-husband's imminent succession to the throne being two of them.

'He will need to find someone to replace me as his wife. Someone willing to look past his behaviour and provide him with an heir too.'

Something she'd been unable to give him and something at the time she'd seen as another of her many failings. Now, of course, she saw it as a blessing, because to have a child caught up in all of this… She shivered and wrapped her arms around her middle, and Hugo's eyes dipped, a crease forming between his brows as his hands flexed at his sides.

'Do you want to change, and we can talk? I can wait here.'

'No, it's fine.'

He nodded, though his frown didn't ease. 'So, you think the Prince might have had a hand in this—this photograph?'

'I don't know. Maybe. Perhaps.'

'I assume he knows you're staying here.'

'There's not a lot the Prince doesn't know about me. He has his *spies* everywhere.'

'Then he will also know this is nonsense.'

'So long as it works in his favour, he doesn't care about whether it is true or not.'

'In which case, we'll make it work in our favour too.'

'I really don't see how we can spin this into a positive for us.'

'Everyone loves a good love story, Cassie.'

And then he grinned, and it lit her up from within. 'You of all people should know this.'

And he was right.

Her marriage to the Playboy Prince had been one such adored tale once upon a time.

Which was why their breakup carried such media weight now.

Were ex-princesses permitted a second chance at love?

Even if the first had never been a love story at all...

'But, Hugo, you have two global companies to run. You don't have the time to spend ferrying me around Paris.'

'I will make the time. I will give Eduardo the autonomy to run the company he has been running for long enough anyway. And I will take a long overdue holiday from the hotel group, let Zara, my number two step in. Besides, it will do wonders for business...just think of the headlines... *Cassie Couture and Chevalier Clubs, a match made in heaven*—you couldn't write it better!'

She laughed wholeheartedly now. 'Hugo! I'm not even out there as a designer yet.'

'Not yet you're not. But you will be if I have my way.'

She shook her head, her chill forgotten. In fact, she felt positively balmy. All thanks to him.

'But I am serious, Cassie. Being seen on your arm can only do great things for Chevalier Clubs, so you have nothing to fear for me on a personal or professional level. And, dare I say it, we enjoy each other's company, and it has been a long time since I have taken any kind of holiday, as my latest night-time misadventures prove, so I am long overdue a break too. You will be doing me a favour as much as I you.'

How could she turn down such an offer?

He was handing her the perfect solution to her current nightmare.

A chance to come out with her reputation intact, protect her dream, and get back out into the land of the living…but was it right to bury one falsehood with another?

And what choice do you have? The Prince threw you to the wolves the second you dared to leave. It's time to push back. Play them at their own game.

'What's that look about?'

'I've never been…*bad* before.'

He gave a low chuckle. 'It's not all that bad, Cassie. You're divorced. Very much single. I'm single in case you need that clarified.

There's nothing wrong with us dating. Nothing to say we didn't meet here in this very building—which we did by the way—then hit it off and chose to date. Like millions of people do every day.'

'And you're okay pretending be in a relationship with me?'

A curious spark came alive behind his eyes. 'It would be an honour to escort you around Paris as your friend, and if the world wants to read more into that, then so be it. But if, on the other hand, you wanted to present us as more than that or even go as far as to make a formal statement about us dating, I will do that too. Your wish is my command.'

And now she laughed. Because this truly was crazy. And fun. And no matter what he said, it still felt bad. Very, *very* bad.

'But if it makes you laugh like that…' He took her hand in his and squeezed, the look in his eyes stealing her breath away. 'I refuse to believe there can be any bad in it.'

And maybe Hugo was right.

One thing was for sure, it was time she got back out in the world. As her. The *real* her.

Not Cassandra, Princess of Sérignone.

But as Cassie. Fighting for the life *she* wanted. Nobody else.

And with a little help from Hugo, her very hot, very capable next-door neighbour and new-found friend, that feat didn't feel so impossible any more.

CHAPTER FIVE

'YOU READY?'

Hugo hadn't known it was possible to nod and shake your head at the same time, but Cassie had just perfected the move. And the sight amplified his guilt.

The similarity to Sara had been disconcerting before…with their public-facing roles, controlling families, lack of freedom. Poised yet shy. Quiet yet teasing. Kind too.

And to find himself in this position again.

With Sara it had been his fault. He'd thought their love worth outing, worth fighting for, and then he'd almost got her killed.

With Cassie, he had taken her already troubled situation and piled on a whole heap more. And Cassie was right, it wasn't his fault, but it didn't make the situation any better.

And he was determined to make it better.

He was determined that this time, he would get it right.

He would see to it that she was okay. That she would come out of this situation better for knowing him. Not worse.

'It's going to be okay.' He took hold of her hand. 'We have the best security detail looking out for us. A path has been cleared and all you have to do is smile and wave.'

'All?' She gave a tremulous smile, touched her free hand to the braid that fell over one shoulder. It looked simple but he'd warrant she'd spent hours making sure she'd perfected the casual look this morning. The pale pink sweater complemented her English rose complexion. The skinny jeans, knee-high boots, tailored coat and beret gave off every bit the Princess on tour vibe, whether she wanted to or not. Because she had a regal air about her that was all natural. Something her family and the Duponts would have bled dry.

'Or you could do the classic?' he said, pushing away the thoughts that would have seen his fingers crushing hers.

'And what's that?'

'Pretend they're all naked.'

She laughed. 'I thought that was a presentation technique.'

He shrugged. 'Whatever works, right? And once we arrive at the Louvre you will only have eyes for the museum and the architecture anyway.'

Vincent stepped forward. 'The car is ready, Monsieur Chevalier, Princess.'

Cassie's hand tensed around his. He knew she hated the title. But he also knew it was going to take time for the world to drop it. She was their beloved princess, whether she wanted to be referred to as such or not. If she could only see that it came from a place of affection rather than being a cold-hearted stereotype.

No matter the names being thrown about, the slander coming out of the palace, and the trouble Prince Georges was determined to stir up following *that* photograph. It would take more to ruin the woman most of the world at large adored.

And Hugo would do his best to see to it that they continued to adore her.

By fulfilling this role for as long as she required it.

He'd done some extra digging into the Prince of Sérignone, and the more he'd learnt, the more his protective instincts had kicked in. The idea that the Prince had once had any claim over her riled him enough. The fact he now dared to ruin her from afar to save his own face...

Hugo fought the tension coiling through him anew. But the deceit it took to behave like so, the duplicity and the cowardice too. The nerve of the man to transfer his own crimes onto her.

'Hugo?' Her soft prompt brought him back to his senses.

'Shall we?' He released her hand to offer out his elbow, and she gave him the coy smile the cameras knew well. The smile he knew to be as genuine as she was because she *was* nervous, but she wasn't backing down. The nod she gave him now devoid of its contradictory shake.

'Let's go.'

They stepped through the revolving door together and the wall of noise instantly upped, threatening to press them back. He'd anticipated it, of course he had, though nothing could have prepared him for the reality. And though he had worked in the field many years ago, this felt different. But then it was different. This was personal.

And for a split second, he was in another country, another place, another time. And there was another woman beside him. A cold sweat broke out across his skin, the world closed in.

Cameras were going off. Blending with the shouts.

A gun. A man.

He turned.

Left. Right. Ahead. *Bang!*

'Boss.' It was the driver in his earpiece, grounding him in the present. 'Are you good?'

Focus. Focus.

His people were doing their job; they were keeping the crowd back. The car was straight ahead. Everything was good. They were waiting for Cassie and him to deliver the agreed smile, a wave, and then he ushered her into the car.

'Are you okay?' He didn't waste a second to ask.

'Are you?' She blinked up at him. Concern glittering in a sea of green. The black interior all around and the smell of leather, a reassuring cocoon.

'You think to ask me that?'

'I'm used to this, but you…'

He checked her seat belt was secure before fastening his own. 'I know this scene well enough.'

'They were calling your name as much as mine.'

They were also 'name-calling,' but he didn't

feel the need to point that out. Not when she could hear it for herself. And though those names were only few and far between, they were the ones that would've landed the loudest and the hardest.

'Drive on,' he urged their driver, his chest too tight for comfort.

'It wasn't as bad as I feared.'

His eyes snapped to hers. 'No?'

Was she mad? Delirious or on something?

She smiled up at him. 'No. Though you're making me question myself now.'

Yes! He mentally cursed. *Get a hold of yourself. You were the one taking a trip down memory lane. Not her. Dieu Merci.*

'You were exceptional.' He righted his jacket, gave a brusque nod and a smile. 'As calm and as regal as a—'

'Don't say it, please.'

'*Désolé*. You took it in your stride, Cassie. No one will have known that inside you were feeling any different… I'm glad you found it okay.'

'That's because you were there.'

She met his eyes, her own big and wide, her vulnerability genuine and tugging on his heartstrings. Strings he never left exposed. Not since Sara—

And that's why you're freaking out now. And you're supposed to be making her feel better. Not worse.

'You and your team.'

He took her hand in his once more and gave it a squeeze.

'Good, because you're stuck with us for the foreseeable.'

He held her gaze as the vehicle pulled away from the hotel, the camera flashes hammering against the blackout glass and the noise of the reporters muffled by the whirring in his ears. She truly was stunning. Her smile, her eyes, her trust in him…

He had this…didn't he?

He could keep her safe and give her a glimpse of the life she deserved.

And what about you? And your heart? And those strings you never leave exposed?

It was a short drive to the Louvre. Nowhere near long enough to ease the tension that had built throughout his body with the flashback that had come from nowhere. But he forced himself to appear at ease for her sake.

Now he just had to hope all went smoothly, because he sensed that his skittish kitten was only one pit bull away from scurrying back to Louis's and he was determined to see this day through. The first of many outings he had planned if all went well…

As for his own tension, he'd deal with that later. If he had to go ten rounds in the ring with Mickie, he'd do whatever it took to exorcise that demon once again.

And be there for Cassie now.

Cassie had felt the impenetrable shield form around her the moment they had left the hotel.

And for someone who had spent years behind a security detail, indeed being directed by one, this felt different. And she knew that was down to Hugo. Something about this great big bear of a man, with warm eyes and a strong sense of honour, made her feel like nothing could hurt her.

No camera flash or threat from afar. No snide remark or snarky look.

Never had her family or the Prince made her feel quite so invincible.

With her head held high, she walked the grounds and the halls of the Louvre, in awe of its beauty and its art. Its history and its majesty. And it was wonderful. To breathe in the air and the space and be amongst the people too.

They'd even paused and conversed with a

few groups. Taken an extended break when Cassie hadn't been able to resist a group of children who had likened Hugo to a real-life superhero. And he'd spent at least twenty minutes 'flexing' his muscles to whatever feat they had devised. Something their teacher had indulged since they were on their lunch break. Though Cassie got the impression it had more to do with Maîtresse's pleasure than the children.

'I think she liked you...'

'Huh?'

'The teacher...are you *blushing* Hugo?'

'*Non.*'

She paused, forcing him and his team to pause too as she peered up at him. 'Yes, you are.'

'I do not blush.'

She pursed her lips. 'Whatever you say, but for the record, I'm more than happy to share the limelight.'

And he chortled at that, clearly pleased to have her so at ease.

Because she was at ease. Surprisingly so.

She couldn't care that the headlines that morning had been less than kind. That they had smacked of the Prince's skilled spin doctors. She was living in the moment, thanks to him. And the more she thought about his whole idea, the rules of supply and demand, it really did make sense.

'This really is wonderful, Hugo. Truly. Thank you.'

'You're welcome. Now, are you hungry?'

Was she? She hadn't thought about food at all. Her senses were too busy being overloaded by the sights, sounds, and scents of Paris, having spent the last month cooped up in Louis's apartment. But she must be.

It had been many hours since breakfast— a coffee and the smallest dollop of yogurt on fruit had been all she could manage with the nervous churn, courtesy of the headlines.

'I reckon I could eat.'

'That's lucky.'

'Lucky?'

To their left, a grand doorway had been roped off and a liveried footman bowed his head to them both.

She frowned. 'Hugo, what's this?'

'I believe it is the location for dinner.'

'In the Louvre? But the restaurant is back…'

'I thought you might enjoy some privacy for our meal.'

'But I thought the whole point was to give them more and they will demand less?'

'But I'm also a firm believer in balance. There will be a gazillion photos from this morning, Cassie. Now *this* is for you.'

He placed his hand in the small of her back, and she caught the sudden gasp that wanted to escape. It wasn't like his hand was hot. Or that she could feel his palm's heat through her coat, the cashmere of her sweater or the silk of her camisole but she *felt* it.

'This?' The question was more breath than spoken word.

'You'll see...'

He led her through the door that was now being held open to them. A classical tune played softly through some invisible sound system, and inside, the rich red walls created an intimate backdrop for the table that had been lavishly laid out for two with a gold candelabra adorned with white roses at its heart. And to the side, glass cabinets had been rolled in on wheels, each displaying pieces of art.

She sent him a questioning look, unable to form a word.

'When you've worked in the hospitality industry for as long as I have, you build up an extensive contact list...and the odd favour or two.'

'*This* was a favour?'

He didn't reply, only smiled as she made her way over to one of the cabinets. Hand to her throat because she couldn't believe any of this was real. That Hugo had organised this. It was too much. Too sweet. Too thoughtful.

'I arranged for them to be brought from the Prints and Drawings Study Room. They can only be viewed by appointment anyway, and I thought…well, enjoy.'

She looked down and gave a soft chuckle. 'The Gallery of Fashion by Heideloff… You brought these here.'

He came up behind her. 'Not me *personally*…'

She gave him the elbow. 'Funny.'

'Like I already told you, I don't know much about fashion, but a quick search of the Louvre brought up this collection, and I thought since we're here, it might inspire you with your work and…'

He leaned over her shoulder to take a closer look, his warmth, his masculine woody scent enveloping her as he did so. She felt her eyes threaten to close, the desire to savour the moment as ludicrous as it was real.

'Though looking at them now, I can see how foolish *that* was.'

She forced her eyes to widen at his sarcasm,

forced herself to take in the beauty of the drawings that were over two hundred years old. 'Hugo! They're of their time, but no less exquisite!'

'Of their time? How you women managed to sit down let alone put one foot in front of the other in all those skirts is beyond me.'

'But look how delicate they are, and who doesn't love a good fan?'

He gave a soft chuckle.

'You laugh, but back then a fan could convey a multitude of secret messages.'

'Right,' he drawled.

'I'm serious! They weren't just a beautiful accessory but a way of communicating with a lover or a would-be suitor…it could be as innocent as declaring your wish to stay friends or as ardent as "I love you".'

She could feel her cheeks warm under his gaze, though she kept her own fixed on the images beneath the glass. They truly were beautiful.

'Seems dangerously open to interpretation to me. I'm a literal man. You've got to tell me how it is.'

She laughed. 'I'll remember that—*not that we're*…'

She let her words trail away with the background music as her blush deepened further. The effect of his body so close behind her, enough to make her feel like he was a furnace in full flame.

'Monsieur. Madam. Dinner is ready if you are?'

An older gentleman entered the room and she sidestepped away, feeling oddly caught in the act. The act of what she wasn't sure. Only that her blush made her look as guilty as she felt. But to have someone other than Hugo address her as something other than princess…to know that Hugo must have had a word…that he had done all of this for her too. She was walking on air and her smile filled her face.

'Favours go a long way,' Hugo whispered in her ear, his hot breath rushing through her veins as his thoughtfulness continued to warm her heart. 'Henri, it is so good to see you again.' Hugo swung away from her to greet him. His handshake and arm clutch the kind one would give an old friend, not an acquaintance delivering on a favour.

'And you, sir. I trust everything is as you wanted.'

'Impeccable, merci.'

She felt the older man's curious gaze drift

to her and she kept her gaze lowered. She was giving too much away. For a woman used to locking her true feelings and thoughts inside, this was definitely too much. But then she wasn't used to someone doing such things for her. Such deep and meaningful things. And she felt overwhelmed. Tearful even.

'And you're sure you want us to leave the food to the side?'

'Absolutely, Henri, we will serve ourselves. We have everything we need.'

And they did, because as the two men talked, another two delivered trolleys laden with food and drink. More than she and Hugo could ever hope to consume in their time here.

'All we require now is privacy.'

'And for that you have come to the right place.'

'Thank you, Henri.'

Henri clipped his heels together and bowed. *'Bon appetit, monsieur...madame.'*

'Merci,' she managed to say with a shaky smile.

'Do you want to help yourself while I pour us a drink?' Hugo said, checking the labels on the bottles. 'Would you like some wine or some champagne perhaps?'

'Champagne would be lovely.'

Because it truly would. And, *oh, my*, she simpered on over to the exquisitely arranged trolley. What on earth was wrong with her? She was used to people going overboard to make her feel welcome when she visited establishments. To serve and to lavish her with the best they had to offer, but this was so different to all of that.

Just as Hugo's protection felt different to all that had come before.

'Are you okay?'

She sensed his frown rather than saw it, because for the life of her she couldn't look at him. Not with the tears in her eyes, and the chaotic race of her thoughts and her feelings.

'Of course. This is incredible, Hugo.' She focused on filling her plate with all manner of delicacies, not that she saw a single one. 'I'm just a little overcome, if I'm honest.'

'But you must be used to such attention? I know you're not used to serving yourself dinner but for the rest...'

She spun to face him. 'No, Hugo!' She placed the plate down before she dropped it, her entire body trembling as she shook her head. 'I'm not used to any of this!'

He paled as he straightened from the table—champagne forgotten. 'Cassie?'

'I'm sorry! It's just too sweet. Too thoughtful. Too—just too much! *All* of it. Georges knew my passion for fashion. And that rhymed and it wasn't meant to rhyme.' She gave a laugh that sounded as silly and as stupid and as ungracious as she suddenly felt. 'But never would he have thought to arrange such a private viewing. So intimate and thoughtful and caring. Yet here you are, knowing me what— a few days? Whisking me up in this…all of this?' She lifted an unsteady hand to gesture around her at the beauty of it all, her eyes misting over. 'It is too much and yet it is wonderful, and I am so grateful and I am so sorry because I am not behaving like one who is grateful should.'

He was across the room in a heartbeat. His hands wrapped around hers. His body— tall, strong, and warm—before her. 'Breathe, Cassie. Just breathe.'

She did as he commanded. Took a breath and another. Looked up into his eyes that were calm and steady and sure.

'It's okay. You are okay. Nothing can hurt you here. No one can hurt you here.'

She shook her head. 'I don't know how I can repay you for this—this kindness you have shown me.'

'You insult me by suggesting that such an act requires payment. This has been a pleasure shared, Cassie. To see you leave that hotel room has been all the payment I need.'

'But it is too much, all of this. You know I have no money of my own. Not yet.'

'I care not for your money but your happiness.'

And there was such strength to those words, such warmth to his touch, his hands caressing her own, his body pressed so close to hers that she felt like she could combust on the spot and would still be the most deliriously happy person alive.

'Apologies, Cassie, yet again I overstep.' He broke away from her, so quickly she staggered back. 'Please excuse me.'

She snatched his hand back, eager to reassure. Eager all the more to make him see that this was more on her than it was on him. It was her own insecurity, her own uncertainty about where her head was at, her life and her heart, to know what was and wasn't okay.

Hell, her friends, those people that she could really trust, were few and far between, and he was so new and so dizzying in the way he made her feel, too.

Feelings that, if she was truly honest, she

had no experience in understanding or trusting, let alone managing.

Especially when she feared that she was projecting those feelings onto him too.

'There's nothing to excuse...' And leaning up on her tiptoes, she pressed a kiss to his cheek. It was fleeting and barely there and very much driven on impulse. 'Thank you, Hugo. For getting me out of the apartment and for all of this. Georges may bear the title, but as far as fairy tales go, you most definitely befit the role.'

And then she turned away before she said anything more revealing, *did* anything more revealing, and focused on the delicious spread of food to devour rather than the man.

Though, if she were given the freedom of choice, she knew in a heartbeat which would win.

CHAPTER SIX

A FEW DAYS LATER, Hugo knocked on Cassie's door.

He'd called ahead to make sure she was up for a day out. Told her to layer up in outdoor exercise gear and left it at that.

She'd been in the public eye a lot over the past week. Following the success of the Louvre, they'd crammed in plenty—the Palace of Versailles, the Musée d'Orsay, Sacré-Coeur—the list went on and the press were spoilt for choice when it came to pictures and stories. Last night's trip to the opera had been particularly romantic and snap-worthy.

Though today was once again about striking a balance, gifting her Paris and some anonymity in one, and it was either going to be a brilliant surprise or an epic disaster. He couldn't wait to find out which.

The security detail could though. Their faces when he'd told them what they'd be doing…he should have recorded it for his father. That would have made the old man laugh.

Not that his parents knew about Cassie yet, because if they'd heard, *he* would have heard. And right now, digi-detox land was gifting him more than just a quiet life workwise, it was protecting him from the third degree on a personal level. Because his mother would be all over this, her excitement unbearable.

Almost as unbearable as his father and his work interference.

He was going to have to get ahead of it and tell them the truth *before* his mother got wedding planning. Though he had a few weeks before they were out of digi-prison—his father's choice of name—and that should buy him some time. He could cross that bridge then.

And he'd just tell them the truth. It was a fake relationship to protect a good woman's reputation. Hell, his father might even be proud of him. They were well protected by the firm. And ultimately, Cassie wasn't Sara, so he wasn't about to make a public fool of himself. They would manage the breakup, when it came to it, with dignity on both sides. No harm, no foul. Simple.

Her door opened and she smiled up at him, all tentative and unsure as she finished tying her hair back into a ponytail. 'Will I do?'

He took a second to steady his heart, another to reply…and even then, he paused to look at her, truly look at her. Taking far too much pleasure in drinking her in, but knowing she wanted his honest opinion.

Was there anything this woman couldn't pull off? She was wearing trainers, socks slouched at the ankles, black leggings, and a sports jacket zipped high to her chin—nothing sexy about it but…

Just tell them the truth, he quoted himself back. *But which truth? That this is a fake relationship or that you find her sexy?*

'Are you windproof?' he said, ignoring the inner taunt as he mentally waved the platonic flag…though he might as well have waved a red rag to a bull. 'We're not due any rain but without any cloud cover the wind has a bite to it.'

'I'll be good.' She pursed her lips. Green eyes sparkling. 'Thanks, Mum. And that's a compliment by the way, because my mum was all about how we looked and *not* whether we caught our death.'

His cheeks warmed while his heart chilled

over the woman he'd now been able to put a face to thanks to one of his late night googling sessions while catching up on some work. Yes, he'd taken some overdue holiday, but there were some things he couldn't just drop last minute, not at his level.

'Of course she was. But just in case, do you have a buff?'

'A what?'

'A neck warmer? Something you can pull up over your face?'

Which would also have the added benefit of concealing her lips from view…lips which seemed to get more alluring and distracting by the day. And how was that even possible?

She unzipped her pocket and pulled out a tube of fleece from her pocket, her smile proud as punch. 'You mean one of these.'

A brusque nod. 'That'll do. Let's go.'

'Wait.' She grabbed his arm as he started to race away, and he had to resist the urge to snatch it back as the connection thrummed through his veins, leaving him craving more of the same. 'Do I need my purse, a drinks bottle, snacks, anything else?'

'Everything else is taken care of.'

She gave him a peculiar look. 'You going to tell me what we're doing?'

'You'll find out soon enough.'

She let him go and closed her door. 'Are you always so mysterious?'

He didn't reply and she hooked her fingers in his as they headed for the elevator. A connection they had come to do so often when in company of late that she obviously did it now, and ordinarily it would be fine. But they weren't in company yet, and there was no one around to put a damper on what she had sent licking along his veins…

'What's that frown for?'

'Huh?'

She was pressing the button for the lift, but her green eyes were very much on him.

'Nothing.'

'Liar. I've not known you very long, Hugo, but I know when you're pensive about something.'

The elevator pinged, launching him back to the discomfort of *that* night and the present moment in one, and he propelled himself inside as soon as the doors slid open, taking her with him.

'Hugo?'

His eyes slid to hers.

Nom de Dieu, she's had enough dishonesty in her life…just give her something.

'If you really must know, I was thinking that I'll have to come clean to my parents about our relationship and the reasons behind it at some point.'

'Oh, goodness, of course.' Her eyes flared up at him. 'I'm sorry I hadn't even considered it. How thoughtless of me!'

'Hey.' He squeezed her hand. 'These are my parents, my concern, and we don't need to worry about them just yet. They're still enjoying my birthday gift, remember? We have a few weeks' grace.'

'You reckon news isn't going to slip through the resort's net?' She gave a dubious laugh. 'I can't imagine any place on this earth being *that* secure.'

'Depends on how desperate you are to get a fix, I guess.'

'Your father strikes me as the kind to get his hands on a phone at the very least.'

'If he does, the last thing my father will be checking is the celebrity news.'

She gave another laugh. 'True. Though are you sure one of your staff isn't going to let something slip about the boss of the hotel chain? Especially when the father of said boss is a guest…'

'I think that makes them all the more likely to be discreet, don't you?'

'You put a lot of faith in your staff.'

'I do.'

She eyed him from beneath her lashes.

'What's that look about?'

She chewed the corner of her mouth.

'Cassie?'

'Did you find out who took the photo?'

He clenched his jaw. He hadn't wanted her to ask because he hadn't wanted to tell her, but he wouldn't lie. 'Yes.'

'And?'

'It's been dealt with.'

'Hugo, please…?'

'She was a young, single mum. Desperate for the money. She passed all the checks, there was no reason for my team to be concerned. Though we can assure you changes are being made to avoid the same thing happening again.'

'I see.' She fell silent for a moment then, 'Did you report her to the police?'

She sounded sad, forlorn, and his mouth twisted to the side as he thought of the young woman's face, the evidence of drug addiction too obvious to ignore.

'No, Cassie. I did not. Vincent has put her

in touch with a women's support group that his wife is involved in. Hopefully getting help that way will set her on a path to a better future.'

She looked up at him, the golden light of the lift sparkling in her emerald depths.

'What's that look about?'

'I'm not sure you want to know.'

'No?'

She shook her head. Her ponytail sashaying down her back and taunting him further.

'Cassie…' It was a low growl and she nipped her lip, eyes still sparkling.

'You really don't, Hugo.'

He reached out and hit the emergency stop button. 'I'll be the judge of that.'

Her eyes flared. 'Hugo! You can't stop the lift.'

'It's my lift, I can do what I like. Now, I gave you the truth, so out with it.'

She lifted her chin, the defiant angle triggering a rush of heat south. 'If you really must know, you give off this Mr Suave Sophisticated Hotelier Tough Guy vibe, but you're as soft as they come, Mr Chevalier. An absolute teddy bear! And you should be out in the suburbs setting up a home with some lovely woman and popping out glorious mini-Chevaliers with hearts as good as their papa's.'

Her finger was pressed into his chest by the time she had finished her little speech. Her cheeks were streaked with the passion of her words and her mouth was parted on her last breath and her eyes held his, fierce and determined.

'Is that so?'

And hell, she could have said anything, done anything and he would have taken it, because in that moment she was glorious, impassioned, and so far removed from the wallflower who had been hiding out in her room that first morning.

'It is so.'

'Monsieur, madame, quel est le problème avec l'ascenseur?'

Hugo looked up at the camera above his head, to where Vincent was likely eyeing them in confusion and gave an apologetic wave.

'Tout va bien, Vincent.'

He sent the lift back on its journey to the basement, where his team were waiting to kit them out with their mode of transport for the day. And counted his lucky stars for the camera keeping watch and his team that would continue to keep watch. All holding him to account that day and every other day, because what he'd been about to do no one should have witnessed.

And his good conscience should not have permitted. He was supposed to be helping Cassie on a journey to a better life, not complicating it.

As for what she'd said, it was so close to what his mother had been begging him for since he'd turned thirty. But as he'd made clear, he had no interest in going there. His relationship with Sara had left him scarred not just physically but emotionally. And whilst the former had healed, the latter not so much. And his mother knew it.

Knew it and still she pressed, wanting him to move on. To find love, to trust and have a family of his own. But you couldn't simply stitch the heart back together. It didn't just heal.

A strange warmth crept along his arm and he looked down to find Cassie's thumb caressing the back of his hand. A mindless caress that had him clearing his throat. Did she even know she was doing it?

The lift came to a gentle stop at the basement level, and he pulled his hand free, raked it over his hair.

'I hope you had a hearty breakfast,' he said, more for something grounding to say as the elevator doors opened and they stepped out.

'You know exactly what I had—you sent it.'

'But did you eat it?'

'I ate— Oh, my God, Hugo! You're kidding!' She came to a standstill, her hands pressed to her cheeks as she took in the van ahead with the bikes, the bags, all the equipment and his team...

'It's not quite running but you said you missed the wind in your hair, the freedom. I figured this was the next best thing. And with the helmets and the clothing, no one will even know it's us sneaking out of here on the bikes.'

'They'll work it out at some point.'

'Let them. I think we rock the exercise gear, don't you?'

She laughed, her cheeks warming under his gaze that was likely ablaze with far too much appreciation and not enough jest.

'And your team are up for this?'

'They're all up for it, aren't you, guys?'

There were a few grunts, a few smiles, even some boisterous lunges from the back. 'We have an inconspicuous mix of runners, cyclists, and a car. We're good. We'll get to see some sights and so long as the weather holds, we'll have a late picnic in the Bois de Boulogne. Maybe even spot a red squirrel or two.'

Before he could say anything else, her arms were around his neck, and she was squeezing the very air out of him. 'Thank you!'

'Well, we haven't left yet. This could be my craziest idea so far, cycling and picnicking at this time of year in Paris, but I figured it gave you the best chance of beating the foot traffic.'

She dropped back just enough to look into his eyes. 'See! Teddy bear!'

And then she was racing off to get her bike, and his team were all easy smiles and eager to please because nothing was too much trouble when Cassie was in the room. Nothing whatsoever.

The spell she cast over all around her was as effortless as it was unintentional.

No wonder the Prince was behaving like a man still half mad, a man still half possessed by her…

Hugo had breathed the same air for a week and it might as well have been a year for all he felt overrun by her.

She mounted her white-framed bike and tested out its bell, her laugh lighting up his world, and he accepted that he didn't mind being overrun at all. Not if it meant he was going to get it right this time and she was going to walk away happier for having met him.

And what about you? Are you going to walk away happier? Whole?

But this wasn't about him. This was about her.

Cassie not Sara.

And he had this, he reminded himself firmly. This time, he had it, because he wasn't a man being led by his heart but his head. He was in control. And he would do this to make up for the past and fix the future for a woman who had no one else to fight in her corner for her.

Though if he was honest, he could see her fighting for herself very soon.

Cycling around Paris with Hugo made Cassie wonder why she hadn't thought of getting a bike sooner. With the helmets and all the layers, no one recognised them to begin with. The varying modes of transport meant the team as a whole blended in with the general population, and at their core, they just looked like a group of friends taking a ride out.

And it was amazing. To act the tourist, to *be* a tourist. To be able to stop and take photos, rather than be the subject of them. To have a drink and sample the street food, rather than dine at prearranged times and prebooked establishments.

To see and experience the real Pah-ree!

They weaved their way to the Bois de Vincennes—a sprawling expanse of woodland to the east of the city—and from there he told her they would take the Rive Gauche, the left bank of the Seine all the way along to the Bois de Boulogne, another stretch of woodland to the west. Though if she was honest, as she took in the boats floating on the picturesque Lac Daumesnil, she felt the smallest pang of envy.

'Would you like to do that another day?'

She found him looking over his shoulder at her. Was there anything this guy didn't detect? He seemed as skilled as any one of the bodyguards. The way he scanned a fresh room. The way his body somehow managed to be ahead and behind her all at once. The way he seemed to spy a potential problem before the team could fully express it.

There was the feeling of being safe and protected because of Hugo, and then there was the feeling of being all warm and fuzzy and cherished because of Hugo.

And that's where things got tricky...

'I wasn't expecting so much hesitation after such a smile of longing.'

She gave an abrupt laugh. 'Don't you have a job you need to get back to? You've already taken a week out to show me the city.'

And now she just sounded ungrateful.

She bit her cheek and winced.

'Eduardo is thriving now he's off the Chevalier leash. And Zara, once she picked herself up off the floor, is very grateful to have been entrusted to run things in the hotel group for a while. Your appearance in my life couldn't have come at a better time it would appear.'

'To be considered a blessing when I've been something of a distraction...' She shook her head. 'I never thought I'd hear that one.'

He slowed his bike so that he was alongside her, his piercing blue eyes seeking out hers, which she purposefully kept averted. 'That wasn't what you were thinking about though, so stop trying to distract me and spill.'

'You need to keep your eyes ahead Mr Chevalier, else you'll end up in the lake *today*.'

'Are we back to titles, Princess?'

She winced. He was right. And she knew why she'd done it. She was hiding behind the respectful form of address, using it to create distance between them, which wasn't fair. Not when he had done nothing wrong, and everything right. Not when she was purely protecting herself by pushing him away, inflicting hurt in the process, and that wasn't on.

'Sorry, Hugo. Consider me told.'

'I don't need you told. I just need you to stop it.' He smiled. 'And you don't need to tell me where your head has gone, not if you don't want to. Your private thoughts are your own and I'll respect that.'

She shook her head. 'It's just… Why are you doing this, Hugo?'

'Because I want to.'

He sent her a guarded look that she so desperately wanted to rip apart and understand. Regardless of the privacy he had just granted her. Which she knew was about as unfair as her pushing him away, and still she pressed. 'But why?'

'Because I couldn't bear the thought of you trapped another day inside that apartment with all of this on your doorstep.'

'I would have got out eventually.'

'And that's the problem—*eventually*! Life's too short to live your life like that. Trapped by what you can't control.'

'So, you thought to lure me out?'

'I figured it was high time you had yourself an ally, someone to fight in your corner with you… Is that so bad?'

'No.'

'And I'm afraid it's in my nature. You speak to my mother and I was always one for bringing home the stray and injured when I was a kid. Not that I'm comparing you to the stray and injured,' he hurried to add when she gave a choked laugh. 'But I'm serious…if you ever meet her, she'll likely tell you the tale of the water boatman I tried to save from drowning, not that I knew what he was at the time.'

She frowned. 'Water boatmen. But don't they…?'

'Swim. Yes. I soon learnt as much. Once she got over her fit of the giggles.'

'Oh, Hugo, you really are a—'

'No more teddy bear, please. It's bad enough

that my father always accused me of being too soft. And I was four.'

'Yes, and now you're a full-grown man…'

One sexy specimen of a man who she had all these feelings for, and she didn't know what to do with them or whether he felt them too. And that was scaring the hell out of her. Not that she was about to tell him that.

'And you have a company to run and friends you must want to spend time with. A family too. You shouldn't be out here, spending all your spare time with me.'

'I told you, my parents are on their retreat, and yes, I have friends of which you are now one. As for work, a perk of being the boss is that I get to choose when I do it, which is something I've forgotten in recent years. Besides, this is kind of working, getting to see this side of the business that I've not been a part of in so long.'

'But I'm not paying you.'

And what did he mean—*a part of in so long*? Had he worked for his father? And when?

'See it as extra training on their part.'

'And do they need it? The extra training?'

He grinned.

'Hugo?'

'We only employ the best, Cassie.'

And there was her answer…he wasn't boasting, he was simply stating a fact. And she admired him for it. Her gaze swept over every chiselled feature in his stocky frame, which somehow managed to look lithe and athletic as he pedalled beside her.

'I'm sure you do.'

'But the best always leave room for improvement.'

She snorted. 'My father would see that as some kind of ridiculous riddle never to be solved.'

'Impossibly high standards?'

'You could say that.'

'And your mother?'

'You know the saying, if you can't say anything nice, don't say anything at all?'

'Oui.'

'I think she makes it her mission in life to live by the opposite.'

'Oh.'

'She's a delight.'

They fell silent as the path narrowed into single file for a stretch before widening once more and he was back alongside her.

'I was thinking about how safe you make

me feel, Hugo. Just now,' she blurted before she could chicken out a second time. 'When you asked. It's not just about your team, the security detail, but it's you, how thoughtful you are, how your presence is like this shield that's several times your physical size, and it…it feels good.'

Heat bloomed in her cheeks and she hoped he'd attribute it to the exertion and not the extra kick to her pulse that her confession had triggered. Though maybe it was as simple as what Hugo himself had said. That he *was* her ally. Her champion. That for the first time in her life, she had someone to encourage her to go after what she wanted for a change. And it felt good.

It didn't have to mean she was starting to have *feelings* for him. Messy. Complicated. Feelings. That ran deeper than friendship.

'*Bien*. That makes me happy.'

'You said something just now, something about seeing this side of the business after all this time…does that mean you used to work for your father?' she found herself asking, needing the focus off her, but also wanting to understand what he'd meant. Whether he'd tried it out and walked away at some point.

Whether, like her, he'd chosen to break away from the expectations of others.

'I did,' he said after a long pause. 'Many years ago.'

He didn't look at her now, the tension in his jaw telling her he wasn't happy with the change in topic. She wanted to press, but she also wanted the man at ease back.

Ahead, the art deco masterpiece that was the Palais de la Porte Dorée came into view— something she'd only previously glimpsed from the speed of a passing vehicle. She wanted to stop and take a closer look. The National Museum of Immigration History was something that truly interested her, but she also knew that as soon as their helmets came off, the anonymity they were enjoying would swiftly be gone.

The noise of the traffic built as they came to the edge of the park and they slowed to a stop in silence. Took a drink.

'My father is a hard man to please,' he surprised her by saying. 'I had to do more than prove myself before I joined his company. I had to prove myself above and beyond those that he employed, because heaven forbid it looked like he'd given his son a free ride.'

'Would you have had it any other way though? Truthfully'

He gave a soft huff, took another slug from his bottle. 'I would have taken a kind word occasionally, some encouragement… I guess I resented it at the time.'

She frowned. 'The fact that he made you work for it?'

'No, not that. But the fact that he made me feel like nothing I ever did was good enough. Until one day something changed, and he saw me. Congratulated me. Welcomed me in.'

'And let me guess.' She smiled as she thought about how much that must have meant to him, meant to them both. 'By that time, you were better than all the rest?'

He gave a tight chuckle. 'Are you going to break out into song for me?'

'God, no. You never want to hear me sing.'

'I'll be the judge of that.'

'So, what happened?'

His eyes wavered as they stayed connected with hers, shadows chasing behind his eyes that she couldn't read.

'You ready to go again?'

No, she wanted answers. But she could wait until he was ready. He'd gifted her so much of his precious free time, after all.

She nodded, and they eased off. Falling into single file as they hit the busier streets of the city and though the traffic made conversation impossible, she was no less happy. No less grateful too, because she was out in the fresh air, seeing Paris the best way possible thanks to him.

Her teddy bear made of steel...

CHAPTER SEVEN

'ARE YOU WARM ENOUGH?'

The late-afternoon sun hung low in the sky. Its orange glow more visual than effective at keeping off the chill now that they'd swapped the bikes for the picnic rug. And though their spot beside the lake was sheltered from the wind by the trees and the general public by his team, he was starting to question his choice to dine outdoors.

The autumn chill did mean less of an audience though, which also meant less chance of an unwarranted intrusion and therefore more pleasure for her. Or so he would have thought. But she'd fallen unusually quiet through their meal. Her gaze on the lake turning distant. And, yes, Lac Inférieure, with its pretty little island and its rounded monument dedicated to Napoleon III, deserved to be looked at, but he got the impression she wasn't seeing any of it.

'I'm fine.' She snuggled deeper into the blanket he'd wrapped around her, the curve to her cheeks giving him a hint of the smile beneath. 'I'm more than fine. This has been the most perfect of days. Right up there with the Louvre.'

He cocked a brow. 'A day of cycling…many would see that as some kind of torture.'

'You knew I wouldn't though.'

'That's true enough. And yet you seem a little distant now that we're off the bikes… was it too much food? I warned Lucile you ate like a bird.'

Now she was the one cocking a brow as she eased out of the blanket cocoon to give him the full weight of her unimpressed stare. 'A bird?'

'A bird with very discerning taste.'

That earned him a laugh. 'Sorry, old habits and all that. I'm getting better. Moderation is your friend. Mum was all about the slippery slope growing up.'

'Hence the no sweets and chocolate.'

'You remember me saying that?'

'Of course I remember. Hearing someone say they were forbidden treats as a child isn't something you forget in a hurry.'

'So that's why Lucile provided them in abundance.'

'No, Lucile just likes to do her own thing. Just like you're getting to do these days.'

'Well, you can tell her it was delicious, all of it. And I am pleasantly full and very much looking forward to the cycle back so that I can work it all off again.'

'Oh, no, there's no more cycling today. We have a van returning all of this and we're taking a car back so we're free to enjoy this.' He turned to pull a bottle of champagne from the cool box. 'If you're not too cold for it?'

'One can never be too cold for champagne, surely? Especially in Paris, the city of…' She bit her lip, her cheeks flooding with colour.

'You can say it, Cassie.' He eyed her, wondering why she wouldn't. Was it for his benefit? Was she worried he would get the wrong idea? 'It's what we're here for after all.'

'Only we're not.'

And what did he say to that?

She wasn't wrong. But she wasn't right either. Because the whole point of this pretence was to show the world they were in love. But no one was eavesdropping this second, he'd muted the comms. And visually, *he* was right. They were out in the open. On a picnic rug. Sharing champagne. Any passer-by could snap the classic 'love shot'. So why had she felt the need to say it?

'I'm sorry.' She touched a hand to his arm. Gave an apologetic smile. 'You're right. This looks good. Sets the perfect scene. I was just…overthinking.'

He returned her smile. *Overthinking.* That sounded about right. Because he felt like he'd been treading those murky waters too of late. Questioning things too much. The way he felt, too much. The desire, too much.

He popped the cork, the explosive action too in tune with his thoughts, and she gave a small squeal as it overflowed. 'Was it a stubborn one?'

'A little,' he hurried out, clinging to the excuse she had gifted him as he plucked two flutes from the hamper and offered one out to her.

'Thank you.' She wet her lips. 'You're very good at this, you know.'

'Which bit? The cycling or the opening bottles of wine?'

She gave a soft laugh. 'I was thinking more the romancing.'

He filled her glass before seeing to his own—at least she seemed comfortable mentioning the *R* word.

'We have to make it look believable remember…'

'I think you're doing that very well…it's only been a week and the press are lapping it up—lapping *you* up.'

He grinned. 'Sorry. You can't blame a man for wanting to look good in the process, and if my hotels are taking a boost, all the better.'

'Not blaming you at all, though I apologise now if they start interrogating your exes.' The bottle hit the bottom of the hamper slightly harder than he'd intended, but he didn't make a show of it. 'That's something they can't seem to help themselves with.'

'There isn't much of substance to report on I'm afraid.'

She leaned closer, trying to get a better look at him. 'Explain?'

He shrugged. 'There isn't much to explain, I'm your classic bachelor. I date for fun, nothing more.'

Because the really interesting titbit—the bit the press would love to get their hands on—had been well and truly buried by the people with the power and the influence to make it so.

Much like the remnants of his heart.

'And besides…' He forced a smile, refusing

to let Sara out of the darkest recesses of his mind and into the moment that up until now had been warm and quite enjoyable. 'They'll be too busy reporting on us. Like I said, they love a good love story as much as they love a bad one.'

She gave a tiny shiver and eased her legs up to her chin as she gestured to the path ahead. 'Well, something tells me one of these walkers will have a snap of this out in the world tomorrow.'

'Tomorrow? Don't you mean in the next thirty seconds.'

'Probably.'

'And so long as we're controlling the narrative, it's all good, right?'

She met his gaze. 'Right.'

'And that feels worthy of a toast, don't you think?'

She smiled, green eyes twinkling with gold much like the Eiffel Tower in the distance. 'To us.'

'To us.'

She clinked her glass to his, and he opened up his blanket to her, offering to share his warmth as well as the perfect camera opportunity.

Sure enough, he could sense a snap in the

distance as she snuggled into his side, and he suppressed the twinge of annoyance—he was courting it after all—as much as he suppressed the warmth her body provoked. And focused on what mattered, her and the little bit of her past she had divulged. Because talking about her past sure beat thinking about his…

'So, tell me, was it just your mother's controlling influence or society's in general?'

'Hmm?'

'The eating habits…'

'I don't know. I guess it's easy to blame others when really, the true person to blame is yourself. I should have been stronger. If I wanted the cake, I should have eaten the bloody cake.' She gave a tight laugh, shook her head. 'Yes, my mother watched over me, made sure I was always careful, always knew how many calories were in what. I knew from a very young age that every delicacy came with a price, and hell, the press never let you have a day off. But maybe I shouldn't have cared so much about what they thought in the first place. And then maybe it wouldn't have hurt so much when they turned their back on me.'

'Your parents never deserved to have you as a daughter.'

'On that, I think they will now agree. After the shame I brought on them...'

He squeezed her into his side, his jaw pulsing. 'They did that to themselves when they backed you into a very public marriage with a man who no more deserved you than they did.'

'Not how they see it.'

'That's their problem, not yours.'

'I guess it is. I guess it's also the difference between you and me. Railroading me into the future they wanted for me is a move they will live to regret, whereas for your father, I can't imagine he will ever regret choosing you to take on his firm.'

Oh, there was a time...

'Do you really want to talk about families when we're in this amazing parkland, red squirrels playing at your feet?'

'Red squirrels. Where?'

He dipped his head to a spot in the distance. Nothing but fallen oak leaves now lay at the base of the trees but there had been a red squirrel not so long ago...it wasn't a complete lie. But she knew.

She nudged him with her elbow, the contact as provocative as the truth tightly packed inside his chest. Just not in the same way. 'Hugo!'

'I made him regret it.' He ground out. 'Once.'

It came out as raw as it still felt. Because *he* regretted it. The pain. The foolish act. The stupidity. He stared at where their glasses almost touched, watched the bubbles rising in the glass, but his head had travelled back. Reliving the past as she searched his face and likely saw it all.

'When?'

'When I worked for him all those years ago… Carving out my own path and going into the leisure industry wasn't entirely by choice, Cassie.'

'No?'

'No.'

She shivered and he pulled her closer. Kissed her hair on autopilot. 'In my defence, I was young. Twenty-four. It was my fifth close protection detail. But even then, I should have known better.'

'What happened?'

'I made a mistake. One I would never be so stupid as to make again, but my father wasn't a man you ever got to disappoint twice.

Though when you're in the business of close protection, such a hard rule saves lives.'

'Did someone get hurt? Did you...?'

She looked up and he tucked her back under his chin, unable to look her in the eye as he admitted, 'I got involved with the principal.'

He sensed her tense, her soft gasp barely audible as he eased back on the rug and she came with him.

'Her father was a head of state in a country where culture and custom would prohibit any sort of a relationship between us, and that was before you put my job into the equation...'

He was so grateful that he'd killed the comms with his team before they'd sat down, grateful all the more for the twenty-foot safety perimeter that meant no one could overhear his shameful tale.

He'd thought he was over it. He'd endured the therapy. Relished the recovery.

Yet here he was, retelling the tale over a decade later, and it felt as raw as if it was yesterday. The heartbreak. His father's disappointment. It didn't matter that he was a billionaire hotelier now, his father's firm under his wing too. He felt transported back to that moment. The twenty-four-year-old son who had broken his father's trust and his own heart in the process. Lost. Susceptible. Weak.

'What was her name?'

Her soft request pulled him back to the present. So typical that Cassie would want to put a name to the face that she didn't know because it mattered to his past.

'Sara.'

'I take it her family weren't very happy when they found out?'

His mouth twisted into a derisive smile, because of course that's where her head would go based on her own experience.

'They had every right to be angry. Cultural and family expectations aside, I was supposed to be protecting her. Love shouldn't have come into it.'

'And did you love her?' she said quietly.

He threw back his drink, but it tasted bitter, unpalatable, or was that just the memory?

'Hugo?'

Answer her.

'I thought I did, at the time.'

'And did she love you?'

'She said she did.'

He took another swig and realised his glass was empty. Reached for the bottle and topped himself up. Went to do the same for her only hers was still full. Not a good sign. He tried to relax. Took a breath. This was ancient history. Dealt with. Though, as he had discovered in the last week alone, it wasn't as buried as he wanted it to be.

His heart too was beating far too close to the surface.

'Then what happened?'

He ground his teeth. He didn't want to go there. But refusing to give it airtime was as bad as admitting it still hurt…

'Her family forced her hand. She made her choice and it wasn't me.'

Whatever she heard in his voice had her hand reaching up to cup his cheek, her palm soft, her green eyes softer still. 'I'm so sorry, Hugo.'

But that wasn't everything, was it? She wouldn't be so sorry when she knew how he had failed Sara. How he had let his heart get in the way of his head.

He was back on that street, Sara's car waiting, door open. The heat suffocating. The look in Sara's eyes all the more so as he caught at her wrist. Desperate. Helpless. Weak. *'Don't go.'*

'Hugo?' Cassie took the glass from his limp fingers, returned to cup his cheeks, her thumbs gently stroking. Her face so close he could see the ring of fire around her pupils. Could see his pain being reflected back at him in the swirling sea of green—and *this* is what love did. *This* is why he never wanted to go back there.

And Cassie was giving him all this compassion when he deserved none.

'It's okay, Hugo.'

He grabbed her wrists, almost threw them down before realising how it would look to a passer-by. How it would feel to her too. An outward sign of rejection that *she* didn't deserve.

'No. It is not.'

'It wasn't your fault.'

'What I did, that was my fault.'

She searched his gaze, unflinching from the pain she could see there. It was the first time she'd witnessed it within him. Such hurt. So raw and unguarded. He had loved. Hugo had loved. More than she ever had.

And he hadn't denied it either. *'I thought I did, at the time.'*

Though Sara had crushed it. Walked away. Chosen her family over him.

Cassie couldn't imagine it. No matter how

hard she tried. Cassie couldn't imagine having the heart of the man before her and choosing anything but that. Though he wouldn't have been the same man…at twenty-four he would have been young, untainted by the world and all the work that would have hardened his shell since. The heartbreak that would have toughened him too.

And she needed that reminder. She needed it now because every day in his company, every day they played out this charade that was their epic love story, she could feel herself getting as lured in as the press. Lured in by him and his kind gestures, his kind smile, his kind heart.

Because it couldn't be so easy as this, could it? After a life of living for others, an adulthood of having her men chosen for her, she couldn't be so lucky as to have landed her own perfect love story right next door. To believe that would truly be naive, wouldn't it?

And she'd almost given herself away too.

It's why she'd blurted out. *'Only we're not.'*

Hugo hadn't needed the reminder. Cassie had.

Her *heart* had.

'By falling in love? I can't see how that's your fault, Hugo.'

He stiffened. 'No,' he ground out. 'But leaving her exposed was.'

The chill ran from him into her and she lowered her palms from his face, rubbed them together. 'I see.'

'No. You don't.'

'Then make me see. Tell me what happened.'

He kept his gaze fixed ahead, but she could see his self-loathing, the sickness in his pallor, and she tucked her hands between her legs, forbade them from moving. He didn't want her touch right now, no matter how much she wanted to give it to him.

'You don't need to tell me, not if you don't want to, but...'

His throat bobbed as he swallowed, his dark lashes flickering over his eyes that were so haunted she prayed that talking about it would in some way release the ghosts from his soul. Ghosts he must have had buried deep for so long.

'I lowered my guard. I was focusing so much on her, fighting with her to see a different future for us that I didn't see the threat until he was upon us. I had my hand around her wrist, I wasn't prepared and when he drew his gun, she was completely exposed.

The only thing I could do was throw myself into it.'

She failed to suppress a shiver as it played out in her mind's eye. 'You threw yourself into the path of the bullet?'

'He never should have got that close.'

'But you did what you were trained for,' she whispered.

'Far too late.'

He raised his hand to his shoulder, scratched at the skin beneath, the scar that must exist and Cassie tracked the move. 'If he'd been any further to the left, or if I'd been any slower…'

She felt the tremor that ran through him with his breath. 'But you weren't.'

He shook his head, stressed, 'He *never* should have been able to get that close.'

'But you were there. And you saved her.'

'I took the bullet but—' he choked on thin air '—it was not my finest moment.'

'We all make mistakes, do things we're not proud of, but you were in love—'

'I was a fool.'

He sounded so angry, so hurt, so bitter, and Cassie's heart ached for him. She could think of nothing else to do but to fold into him, moulding her body into every hard ridge of his until the tension gradually seeped from his limbs. So grateful to have him here now. That he hadn't lost his life in the line of duty to the woman who hadn't loved him enough to keep him.

'I'm so sorry, Hugo.'

'I'm not. Like I said, the only time I let my father down was when I was distracted and infatuated. I learned from that mistake, and I've been committed ever since. Proved myself to my father. Made myself into the man I am today. As for the press, you needn't worry about them digging this story up. Sara's family made sure there was nothing to discover. Nothing to ruin their reputation and her marriage potential back then, and I've told no one of it…my family certainly don't speak of it, and those at the firm are under NDAs.'

She lifted her head a little. 'You think I'm worrying about any of that?'

He gave a stilted shrug.

'I'm more concerned that your relationship with Sara has seen you walk away from the possibility of love in your future, Hugo. This is why you don't have a home in the country with those mini-Chevaliers I mentioned, isn't it?'

He stroked the hair away from her face. 'You make that sound so tragic, Cassie.'

'Because it is tragic.'

He gave a choked laugh. 'Love isn't for everyone. *Mon Dieu*, if you saw my parents… it's a miracle they've got to where they have. My mother has the patience of a saint, I'll say that for her. And I'm a better man without it. I don't need someone else to make me feel fulfilled. I don't want to rely on someone else to make me feel whole and happy again, because when you lose that someone, it's like— it's like having your soul ripped out, and you struggle to see the path for the pain of it.'

'I understand why you don't want to rely on love to make you happy again,' she whispered eventually. 'It's not all that different to me spending my life tying my happiness to that of others. My parents, Georges, things you can't control. But… I don't know. To swear oneself off it because you fear losing it again… I'm not sure that's all that healthy either.'

'I never said it was healthy, Cassie. Just that I don't intend to suffer it again.'

And that was her told.

So why did she get the distinct impression her heart wasn't listening…?

CHAPTER EIGHT

HUGO KNEW PARIS like the back of his hand. He'd grown up in the city. Lived and worked in the good and the bad. Spent time as a driver and on the doors of its clubs until his father had deemed him good enough for the family firm. And then, of course, he'd been launched on the path that had led to his independence.

But he'd never seen it like this…like he did through Cassie's eyes.

And for the next two weeks, while balancing his return to work with his mission to show Cassie off to the world and vice versa, he lost himself in her pleasure, her joy as he took her to his favourite spots, some well-known, some less so.

'I can't believe I'm eating ice cream outdoors when it's almost November.'

Her green eyes sparkled up at him as she touched a finger to the corner of her mouth—*always* smiling—and scooped away some imaginary stray dribble of the sweet delight he had coaxed her into buying.

If he was honest, he couldn't believe he was doing it either. On a Monday too, when he should be at work, but he'd taken one look at the blue sky that morning, the amber leaves on the trees lining the Champs-Élysées creating a stunning walkway all the way down to the River Seine, and he'd known where he'd rather be.

And who he'd rather be with.

And he hadn't questioned it. He'd just gone and got her.

Which in itself was a bad sign to add to the ever-growing list of bad signs…

'I can't believe you've never had one of Pierre's ice creams before.'

'If someone had told me croissant infused ice cream existed down the road, I think I would've sneaked out of my room sooner.'

He had to force his jaw to relax. The memory of her hiding away still too recent to ignore. The gossip headlines that morning, or rather a flippant one-liner from the palace spin doctors, even more so. Not that he was about to ruin the moment by giving it any airtime now.

'It's pretty good, isn't it?' He filled his mouth

with the creamy goodness and focused on the tasty delight instead.

'Oh, yes,' she murmured, her pleasure obvious as she licked at her own, her eyes rolling back. The red of her jacket working with the flush in her cheeks and the gloss to her lips as she swept up the remnants with her tongue...

Don't look at her tongue.

'And the nutty chocolate sauce,' she was saying, 'it really takes it to another level, don't you—'

'Princess! Hugo!'

Her eyes widened as he stiffened.

'Give us a smile!'

The shout came from across the street, and like an echo more shouts followed in quick succession. Other voices, different people.

'Sourire à la caméra!'

It was inevitable. There wasn't an outing where they flew under the radar for its entirety, but his plan was working. The interruptions *were* less frequent. Less intense. Less intrusive. And less insulting with it, too.

Or was that just wishful thinking on his part?

He searched her face, looking for any sign that the unbridled joy of seconds before was dimming. 'What do you say?'

'Do I have food on my face?'

He cupped her cheek, swiped his thumb along her lower lip, felt her subtle tremor beneath his touch—or was that purely within him? The act driven by the thrill of it, rather than to remove any trace of chocolate or cream.

It was the kind of act they'd been indulging in, playing up to the cameras, fulfilling the role of the loved-up couple with ease. Driving the Prince crazy, if the reports were to be believed, and sweeping the public up in their love story. Winning them over to Cassie's side. As it should be.

The only problem was training his body to calm down, reminding it that this wasn't the real deal—because A, he wasn't in love. And B, he never would be.

Which meant *this*—the sexual attraction—it needed to be caged.

'All gone.'

He wondered if she noticed the husky edge to his voice. Noticed it and knew its cause, like he did. That this pretence, the desire, was no act at all.

But her grin widened, and she leapt up, her eyes flashing with mischief as she caught the tip of his thumb in her mouth. *Mon Dieu.*

Never mind the cameras going wild, his entire body surged—heart, mind, and soul—urging him to tug her body to his and kiss her deeply. An act they hadn't been so bold as to share, and it was that deep-rooted desire that had him slipping his arm around her waist and urging her into walking instead.

Because if they were moving, they couldn't be doing all the other things his brain was fervently entertaining…

'You okay?' She leaned into him as she asked, her body readily moulding into his as they fell into an easy step together.

'Better than okay. It's a glorious day. Even the river looks more blue than brown today… which feels like something of a miracle.'

'*Everything* looks and feels a little better when the sun comes out to play.'

He glanced down at her, his brow creasing. 'And are you needing the sun today, Cassie?' Because the wistful note in her voice told him that she did.

Had she seen the same headlines, was she too pondering what her no-good ex would say next. Did he raise it, or did he let it go?

'Are you enjoying your bit of rough, Princess?'

The voice came out of the trees up ahead,

but no one stepped forward and he nodded to his team to check it out as he slowed their pace.

'Do you want to comment on the suggestion that Prince Georges was always a little too refined for you, Princess?'

Hugo saw red. His emotions a sprint ahead of where they should ever be, and not in defence of himself. He couldn't care what the guy said about him. He was lowering Cassie to Hugo's level. And hell, he could say what he liked about Hugo but Cassie...

She tugged on his arm. Her steady hand holding him back when he would have launched forward as the smug-faced journo peered out from between the trees.

'I beg your pardon?' Cassie stepped forward, her hand still on Hugo's arm urging him to hold his ground. Was his skittish kitten finding her claws?

His team in the wings looked to him and he silently gestured for them to hold their position. They were close enough to move if she needed them, but she wanted to handle this, and he wanted to give her that opportunity.

The man came out of the trees. Dark, shaggy hair. Leathers. A motorbike just behind for a quick exit should he need it. Phone ready to snap a pic. 'I said...'

'Oh, I heard you.' She gave her classic coy smile, a lick of her ice cream as she eyed him up and down. 'I just needed a better visual to do this...'

And then she stuck her cone, ice cream and all, right on the end of his nose.

So swift the man had no time to dodge it.

So surprising all the man could do was gawp back at her like some frozen human snowman.

'What can I say? Georges was probably right. I always did have a more playful side to me, and now I'm all about having fun with my man. Life is for living, after all. Don't you agree, Hugo?'

She turned and beamed at him.

'I think I need to go and buy you another ice cream, *mon petit chaton.*'

She wrinkled her nose. 'Did you just call me...?'

'My little kitten, *oui.*'

She hooked her arm back in his. 'Care to explain?'

'Later.'

She gave him a sparkling smile before turning to throw over her shoulder, 'Oh, and, Mr

Reporter Sir, I hate having to waste anything, so please be a good soul and lick as much of that up as you can. It truly is delicious.'

And then she practically skipped Hugo back to Pierre's.

'Are you going to explain the kitten reference?' she asked as he handed her a replacement ice cream.

He chuckled. 'To be clear, to call one *mon petit chaton* is a common endearment in France so you shouldn't take offence.'

'I wasn't.'

He cleared his throat as he thought back to that first morning in Louis's apartment, when he hadn't known who she was…

'And…?'

'It was something that sprang to mind when I saw you standing in the middle of Louis's apartment that first morning.'

'The morning of the photograph?'

He nodded. The story that had triggered all the rest. 'You were wearing that oversized cream sweater, grey leggings, soft and muted against the garish backdrop. Sweet, but skittish too. Wary of me, I guess. Why I was there? Could I be trusted?'

'I suppose I was.'

'And all around you was this chaos and colour and it made me think of a kitten being set down in a noisy neon nightclub. And then you talked about how you were hiding out, and it reinforced that view.' He swept her hair behind her ear, scanned her face as he saw how far she had come to be the woman before him now. '*Mon petit chaton*, hiding from the world, but not any more. My little kitten has found her claws.'

'Hugo…' She wet her lips, her eyes glistening up at him. 'I don't know what to say.'

'Well don't cry.'

'I'm not. I think that's possibly one of the nicest things anyone has ever said to me.'

'And yet, you're crying.'

She shook her head, blinked the tears away. 'I'm not. I'm—I am angry though.'

'I told you, it's a compliment.'

'Not at you! At the reporter for insinuating what he did.'

'Which bit?'

'That you were unrefined.'

'You took that from what he said?'

'Well, the suggestion was there.'

He gave a low chuckle. 'I really couldn't care less what he said about me.'

'Tomorrow's headlines might make you think otherwise.'

'Something tells me that reporter got what was coming to him, I think the reports will swing very much in your favour.'

'You reckon?'

He grinned, his admiration for her swelling out of his control as he caught another stray hair before it found its way into her mouth with her ice cream. 'Hell yeah, you were incredible.'

She stepped closer, so close her chest brushed his front. 'You truly think so?'

He hooked his hands into the rear pockets of her jeans. She felt good. So very good.

'Cassie, I have seen some fierce take-downs in my career, but that is up there with one of my all-time favourites.'

She laughed, though it sounded strained to his ears, strained with the same kind of heat that was working its way through him. 'Now I know you're exaggerating.'

'I swear on my mother's life. Just remind me never to get on your bad side. Like I said, *mon petit chaton* has found her claws.'

She placed said claw over his shoulder. 'I still can't believe that's how you saw me— *see* me, even.' She bared her teeth and gave a playful little *'raa'* that made him laugh… made him feel more than just the flutter of amusement too. 'But have no fear, I don't plan on wasting Pierre's amazing ice cream a second time around, even if it's on your delightful nose… I will share it though.'

Then she licked her ice cream right beneath his nose before lifting it over his shoulder and kissing him. Whether it was for the benefit of more hovering reporters or for her or for him, he had no clue. And he had no good sense left to question it, or prevent it, because he was lost to it. The touch of her lips against his, the taste of the ice cream and her, a delight like no other. And it was heaven and hell in one.

Heaven because it was sheer bliss, and hell because it wasn't enough. And he wasn't sure it could ever be enough. And he shouldn't be doing it. Taking what she was offering, but he was.

Whether it was fake or not. He was rolling with it. Rolling with it and revelling in it. His hands forking into her hair, deep and hungry. The growl low in his throat, fierce and unrestrained. Because he was finally giving it free rein, the desire that he'd been suppressing for so long. It was vibrating through him. Taking over every part of him, until he realised it wasn't just within him, it was against him, in his pocket between them—his phone!

Bzzzz...bzzzz...bzzzz...

He squeezed his eyes closed, swore he heard her whimper, felt her claws along with the drip of her ice cream down his neck.

Bzzzz...bzzzz...bzzzz...

He cursed and she fell back with what sounded like a sob come laugh. 'Maybe you should get it.'

She pressed her fingers to her lips, her other hand outstretched with the dripping ice cream as she kept her gaze low. *Mon Dieu*, she looked thoroughly kissed. Hair mussed, lips swollen, cheeks pink. He wanted to toss the ice cream, drag her back to the apartment, forget the world and why this wasn't real. Why this couldn't *be* real.

He tugged the phone from his pocket as it cut off, cursing the unknown caller for the unwelcome interruption.

Unwelcome? You should be grateful for the reality check!

He raked an unsteady hand over his hair. Took a breath. And another as he stared at the screen and anchored himself in the present. Who she was. What this was. Why he couldn't pick up where they'd left off.

'Do you need to call them back?' she asked, and he could hear the hesitation in her voice, the uncertainty that their kiss had put there. That *he* had put there. Though she had kissed him, that much was certain. But he hadn't had to kiss her back.

'Unknown number. I'm sure they'll leave a message if it's important.'

She nodded but they remained at some weird kind of impasse. Neither knowing how to press Play again…how to resume… not back in each other's arms though, that was for sure.

Maybe he needed to get back into a steady routine. There was something to be said for the reassuring monotony of the daily grind. Less emotion, less hormonal churn, and more making money and decisions with clear thought and logic.

None of which he had when she was around, not any more. And that was a problem. A big Sara-style problem.

Bigger even. Because he was supposed to be older, wiser, and better than the mistakes of old. His phone gave the solitary buzz of an answerphone message, and like a lifeline now he pulled it out. Nodded to one of his team to step in.

'I'll just check what this is,' he said to Cassie.

'Sure.'

He walked a few strides away and dialled his answerphone, surprised when his father's gruff voice came down the line.

'Call me back, Hugo.'

Ice ran down his spine. Was it Mum? Was she sick? Had something happened?

He immediately dialled the number and his father picked up in one.

A stream of Polish flew at him, so rapid even Hugo struggled to piece it together, but he'd caught enough. Princess. Cassandra. Sara. *Imbecyl*—much like the French *imbécile*. So much for his parents being blissfully unaware in digi-detox land.

'Father, stop.'

'Don't you tell me to stop. I knew we shouldn't have left. I *knew* I couldn't trust you to manage things with me so far away.'

Hugo's chest grew tight with every word. 'It is not what you think.'

'How? How can it not be how I think? When your mother learns of this—'

'She doesn't know?'

That was something at least…

'No. Thanks to this *ridiculous* place she's in cloud cuckoo land.'

'Which is where you should be—not the cuckoo—' Hugo broke off with a curse. This was coming out all wrong. Why did his father always get to him like this?

'Did you honestly think I wouldn't find out?'

'And how did you? You're not supposed to have any contact with the outside world.'

'I abide by my own rules, son. You of all people should know that.'

Hugo raked a hand over his hair, gripped the back of his neck. He'd suspected as much. Hell, even Cassie had warned him his father might do as much. But again, he'd been too distracted by the same to do something about it before now.

'Eduardo says you have a team on her 24-7.'

He huffed. 'Eduardo needs to remember who he works for now.'

'Don't change the subject.'

'I'm not. My CEO should be more concerned with running the company than telling tales to my father, who should no longer be getting involved.'

'When those tales pertain to mistakes my son is making in his personal life which could affect his work life, it's my business to know. I thought you'd learnt your lesson with that disastrous affair. Sara and your silly infatuation almost got you both killed. Or has time made you forget?'

'No, Father. And I don't need the reminder now. This is not the same.'

'Then you best enlighten me because from where I'm sitting, it is precisely the same. She is a client and you are—'

'That is *not* how this is.'

'In what way is it any different?'

Hugo blew out a breath. 'Because we are friends and what you're seeing is all for show, Father. I'm helping her out of a difficult situation.' And then he added because he couldn't help himself. 'But even if we were in a relationship, this is nothing like what happened with Sara. I *run* the company now. I'm not in the field. I'm not running the protection detail. I'm being protected right alongside her. And I trust my team. Just as you trusted them. And now, I need you to trust me.'

The line fell silent. Nothing but the sounds of Paris on Hugo's side of the world and the early-morning wildlife in the Caribbean.

'Please, Father, I promise you, I have it all under control.'

Only you don't...

'For the first time in your life, can you just trust me?'

His father grunted. And then he was gone. And Hugo had no idea whether that was a yes or a no. Much like his entire life.

But he knew one thing for sure, he needed to get it under control. His feelings for Cassie and the entire situation and prove to his father once again that he had this.

And prove it to himself while he was at it.

'Everything okay?'

Because Cassie knew it wasn't.

The moment they had kissed, her world had tilted and failed to right itself again.

Cassie now knew how it felt to be wanted by Hugo. Not the kind of want that was make-believe. Projected or otherwise. The kind that she could confuse because he had been so kind and understanding towards her. Because he cared for her.

No. He'd *wanted* her. She'd seen it in his eyes when he'd called her his *mon petit chaton*. She'd heard it in his growl as he'd kissed her. Felt it in his hands as he'd forked them through her hair. Felt it in his body as he'd pressed against her. And she'd wanted him too.

But she'd also sensed the fight in him. The way he'd pulled away and withdrawn.

The phone call gifting him a get out that she had permitted him to take.

And now the wall was well and truly up and he wasn't meeting her eye.

'Hugo?'

'Oui.' He pocketed his phone, then his hands. 'But something's come up and I need to get back and pack. I have to fly out to New York for a few days.'

'Oh.'

And she really didn't like the way her heart sank at the thought.

'I have some business to take care of out there.'

Of course he did, he had a life with responsibilities. Just because he'd *chosen* to spend most of his free time with her of late didn't change that. But now it felt like he was running. From the kiss. From her.

'When will you be back?'

'I'm not sure. Friday maybe? It depends how it goes.'

She nodded. Tugged the collar of her jacket high around her neck, wishing they hadn't bought the replacement ice cream as her stomach threatened to throw it back up. 'I'll miss you.'

And why on earth had she said that?

His eyes caught on hers. For the briefest second their gazes locked, and then he turned away but took her hand as though softening the move. Gave her fingers a squeeze. 'I'm sure your designs will benefit from the extra attention you'll be able to give them without me around to distract you.'

She interlocked her fingers in his. Cherished the connection as she focused on the conversation rather than the weird dance of her heart that was telling her plenty if she dared to listen.

'You're right. If Louis is to unveil them on the catwalk next February, I need to have them ready soon.'

'Still not up for going it alone then?'

She laughed. 'Not yet I'm not. Our little love story may have worked wonders, but I don't think it's worked that kind of magic yet.'

'Our love story has nothing to do with it, Cassie. I'm talking about you and your designs. I've seen them, remember—they're incredible and the world will think so too.'

'And as you so rightly pointed out, you know nothing of fashion so…'

'But Louis does, and he wants them *so…*'

She gave a small smile as she considered what he was saying…while also acknowledging that he was probably saying it to distract her from whatever else was going on inside his head, and between them too.

Was she reading too much into it? She'd kissed him…had he just been going along with it for her sake, for the cameras, for the role?

Or had she gone too far? Crossed a line in kissing him so brazenly? Maybe she should just ask him outright? Or maybe she was overthinking the whole lot, and it really was work taking him away and she was just being paranoid?

Because the real problem came down to what was going on within her. Her own feelings that she was struggling to contain.

So maybe his work emergency was actually a blessing in disguise.

Some space after all the time they'd spent together. A chance to be herself, the new and energised and fierce her. On her own two feet. Alone. And she'd be perfectly fine and perfectly happy without him.

Because she didn't *need* Hugo. She wasn't *in love* with Hugo.

She cared for him. He was a wonderful human being who'd given her so much joy. Saved her from herself and her self-imposed little prison.

She was indebted to him—that was all.
Nothing more.
Absolutely not.
And she'd prove it.

CHAPTER NINE

CASSIE WAS HUNCHED over the coffee table in Louis's living room, a frenetic energy flowing through her fingers and onto the page. The scratch of pencil on paper as soothing as the classical tune she had playing in the background. The tune similar to what had been playing at the Louvre the first time they'd dined together. When he'd had those cute fashion plates brought in for her eyes only.

Had that really only been five weeks ago?

She felt like so much had changed since then. She had changed. Life had changed.

It was half two in the morning. Her witching hour. A time she hadn't needed. Not since Hugo. But in the past week, she'd found herself getting up again…

He'd said he'd be away for a few days, but it had been almost two weeks since she'd seen him. They'd exchanged messages. Mainly him making sure she was okay and that his team were looking after her. Safe topics.

And what exactly is safe *supposed to mean?*

She nipped her lip and went back to her drawing. More focused. More frenzied. Even though her hand and back protested. She lost herself in the beauty of what she could create and control. And her creativity was soaring, her designs were taking shape. She was almost ready to share them with Louis, who'd been messaging daily for an update. Which made her think of Hugo again and his parting words, to think about going it alone. That Louis's eagerness meant the world would be eager too.

But it was still early days. Even with the great strides she'd made to stand apart from her royal identity, standing beside another man was hardly standing alone…but the idea of standing up there without Hugo?

The pencil fell from her grasp and she shivered as she pulled the sleeves of her robe into her hands and curled back into the sofa. She wasn't cold because she feared going it alone.

She was cold because she didn't want to think of life without Hugo in it.

And *that* scared her.

The problem was, she knew it was an act

for him. The fake dating, the playing up to the camera. She knew he cared for her as a friend, but the rest—the loving touches, caresses, gestures—they were all part of the act. Though that kiss… Her fingers fluttered to her mouth that burned with the memory of it…her heart fluttering too.

Because her heart had been fooled.

And her heart wanted to carry on being fooled because it had fallen for the man who had cared enough to coax her out. Who had cared enough to save her from herself.

And when he touched her, when he looked at her, when he made her smile and laugh and feel special in all the ways he did, planning days out that meant so much to her…activities that not even her husband or her parents would have thought to do, would have understood her *well enough* to do…it felt like more. She *felt* so much more.

And she missed him. *God.* She *missed* him.

Waking up each morning knowing he was so far away, that he wouldn't be calling by that day, or the next… She blew out a breath and stood. Walked to the window and gazed out over the darkened city.

How different it now felt having walked it many times with Hugo. Hugo and his team.

But that couldn't be her life forever. At some point she was going to have to move out, take her own path on her own two feet.

That was the deal. That was what she'd wanted more than anything when she'd first fled the palace. Louis had come to her aid with the apartment, and then Hugo had come to her aid in ways she'd never have had the means or the gumption to pursue. Not in the short term when everything had been so fresh and raw.

She had so much to be grateful for, so why did it feel like something was now missing in her goal for the future?

A gentle knock—knuckles against wood—made her jump. She turned from the glass to squint down the darkened hallway. It came again, slightly louder, but very definite. Someone was at her door. At this time of night?

But who would call now unless it was an emergency, and even then, they'd use the bell or pound a lot harder...? She padded towards it, tightening her robe.

A loud whisper came next. 'Cassie?'
Hugo!
She raced the final few steps, unbolted the door, and threw it open. Would have thrown herself into his arms too if she hadn't had the

last-minute foresight to realise that would be unwise. Unless she wanted him to know *exactly* how she felt about him.

'What are you doing here? I thought you were still in New York.'

'I was. I just got back.'

'Like—' she waved a loose finger and swore her heart was about to soar right up out of her chest '—*just* this minute got back.'

'Oui.'

'And you're knocking on my door *because*...?'

He raised his arms out like it was obvious and she eyed him up and down. He was a sight for sore eyes. Even in joggers and a training top.

'Because in the last month we have done many things, apart from the one thing I told you I would do that first morning we had coffee.'

She frowned. 'Remind me...'

Maybe she was losing her mind. Maybe she'd fallen asleep sketching, and this was some weird, Hugo-starved dream.

'A run! It's your witching hour. And I could hear you moving about in there, so I figured, why not?'

Her face broke into a grin. 'You're serious?'

'I've dressed for the occasion, haven't I? You, however...' His eyes dipped, dipped and heated, and heaven help her, she felt the flush creeping up her chest as he cleared his throat and clapped his hands together. 'Right! I'll give you five minutes to get changed because that gown isn't conducive to any form of exercise.'

'Are you—'

'Shoo-shoo!' He took her by the shoulders and turned her around. 'I'll be right here when you're ready.'

And then he closed the door on her, and she was alone once more. Only this time he was on the other side of it, and she was laughing and shaking and completely abuzz with him.

Hugo was here and he was taking her running.

At two-thirty in the morning!

Was there anything this man wouldn't do for her?

He won't love you, so don't be getting any funny ideas!

She dismissed the sarcastic retort—*hell*, what did she care? Her parents hadn't loved her. Georges certainly hadn't loved her. What was another man to add to the list?

But Hugo was different and therein lay the problem.

He was worth loving.

And, breathe.

Watching Cassie run was extraordinary.

Or was it the act of running with her that was extraordinary? Because Hugo didn't feel tired. He felt fired up. Exhilarated.

He hadn't slept since the previous night in New York and, granted, it was only nine in the evening stateside. *She* was the one who should be tired.

But then he'd barely slept the last two weeks away. His sleep was disturbed, and he'd found himself back on the sleepwalk train. Troubled by his own unease. The past and the present colliding. Worry over how he'd left things. Worry over the future. Over what he wanted. What he didn't want. Worry that her ex would cross the line. That another hack of a journalist would. There was the slightest niggle that one would uncover his past too, and the idea that his tainted past could ruin her…he couldn't bear that.

It didn't matter that she'd shown how strong she was either, he'd still worried.

So, the second he'd heard her footfall on

the other side of the wall, he'd been racking his brain for an excuse to see her. To see for himself that she was okay because the reports from his team simply wouldn't do.

Running and her witching hour had been a spark of desperate inspiration.

But now they were out in the cool night air, he was loving every second.

All the more so, because she was.

Her entire body encased in black Lycra, she was a powerhouse. A petite, lithe powerhouse. Her hair was tied back in a ponytail, her face half hidden by a cap, but her eyes shone out, glittering into the night as she turned to him and grinned.

'This is immense!'

They were crossing the Pont Neuf, the Seine flowing black beneath them, the starry sky above, and if he had to choose a perfect moment in his life, he might have chosen this one. 'I'm not going to lie. It is surprisingly awesome.'

She laughed. The sound giddy and light and nowhere near as breathless as it should be. 'Epic!'

'But you know we do need to turn back if you want to avoid the early-morning risers?'

'I know.' She gave him what could only

be described as a cheeky look. 'You want to race?'

'Back to the hotel? It's almost five kilometres!'

'And?' She broke stride to give him a light elbow. 'You chicken?'

'Am *I* chicken?'

She nodded, eyes goading him beneath the rim of her cap.

'You're on!'

And like that, they were off. Any thought of gifting her a head start forgotten as he realised this woman didn't need it. What was she powered by? Moonlight? The reflective details on her kit taunting him further as they flashed him all the way.

By the time they reached their hotel, he swore he'd got a PB along with a rather unpleasant stitch. He cursed as he came to a halt in the outer courtyard, clutched his side as he struggled to suck in a breath. 'You're dangerous!'

'You can't come to an abrupt stop, it's not good for your heart.' She pulled on his arm, her eyes dazzling in the warm glow of the hotel's lighting. 'We'll take the stairs up. You can jog it off.'

He stared up at her. 'Jog it off?'

She nodded. 'Yup.'

'Did you just "*yup*" me?'

'I guess I did.'

He shook his head, hands on knees. 'Who are you and what have you done with my Cassie?'

'I've got claws now, remember?'

She perfected her cat pose, claws and all, before spinning on her heel and jogging inside, ponytail swinging.

'I've created a monster,' he murmured, pushing up to standing with a laugh. 'Never mind a cat.'

Not that he was complaining. Not in the slightest. He followed her on through to the lobby and to the stairwell. There was one thing to be said for jogging up the stairs behind her, he had the most amazing view of her in Lycra. And, *Dieu*, that did not help. Not one bit. It stopped him thinking about his stitch though.

Probably because his blood was rushing elsewhere.

Two weeks apart was supposed to have dulled this.

Made it go away.

Made it containable.

All it had done was made it explosive.

And if he didn't get out of her orbit like now, he was going to do something profoundly stupid, the kind of stupid his father had cautioned him against, the kind of stupid that had made him run two weeks ago...

'Drink?'

'Huh?'

She had her hand on the door to Louis's apartment. 'I make a mean post-workout smoothie?'

The last thing you need is a smoothie...

Though he found himself saying, 'Sure.'

He followed her in and she stripped off her jacket. Underneath she wore nothing but an exercise bra with her leggings. *Gulp.* She pulled her cap off and tossed it aside, her ponytail swinging free down her back as she set about mixing stuff together in a blender. 'Water?'

'Please.'

At least it was supposed to have been a please. Instead, it sounded like someone was strangling a cat and the look she sent him as she pulled open the fridge said she thought so too.

She tossed him a bottle, which by some miracle he managed to catch, and he twisted off the cap, took a long slug. Wiped his mouth. 'Cheers.'

She set the blender going and the noise was about as loud as his pulse in his ears. She set two tumblers on the side with straws and drummed her nails while she waited for the blender to finish.

Was she as edgy as him? She wasn't looking at him and the way those nails were working against Louis's psychedelic marble, the way every exposed muscle of her torso looked clenched... *Dieu*, he wanted her.

Wanted her more than he could ever remember wanting anything in his life. More than he'd wanted the family firm in his twenties. More than he'd wanted to make his first million. More than he wanted to taste the ice cream on her lips a fortnight ago. And that kiss...

The blender finished its incessant thrum, and she let out a sudden breath, her head snapping up. She'd been lost in her thoughts, too. Had she gone to the same place? Unlikely, but the slash of heat still in her cheeks, across her collarbone...

She reached for the jug and poured the luminescent liquid into the awaiting glasses.

'It tastes better than it looks, I promise.'

She stepped up to him, glasses in hand and as her eyes lifted to his, the world stilled.

Because he knew in that moment that nothing could taste better than her.

That he wanted to *taste* nothing but her.

And that he needed to get the hell away from her.

Now.

'I'm sorry, Cassie, this was a bad idea.'

'The drink?'

But he was already turning away and walking, and she was right on his tail. Drinks forgotten on the side as she grabbed his arm to pull him back. 'Did I do something wrong?'

'No, no, of course not. You could never do anything wrong. I'm sorry, I just…' He turned to face her and she was so close, her body virtually pressed up against him, and they were so hot and sweaty from their run. Everything was in some heightened overdrive. Now wasn't the time to make any crazy decisions or cross any rational lines when there was no press corps to excuse it.

'Then what is it?'

She reached up. Her palm soft against his cheek. Her brow furrowed with concern. But there was something else in her green eyes.

Something so akin to the fire in his gut, and *hell*, he wanted to act on it.

He cursed under his breath, and her luscious mouth quirked to one side. 'You do have a filthy mouth at times, Hugo.'

'If you could read my mind, you'd say I had a filthy one of those too.'

Her eyes flared, the fire he had glimpsed turning into a full-on blaze. 'What are you saying?'

'What do you think I'm saying?'

Her delicate throat bobbed, her eyes raking over his face as her fingers trembled against his cheek. 'Don't tease me.'

'*Me?* Tease *you*? When you're the one standing before me in nothing more than a bra and skintight pants?' His voice was raw— raw with a need that had been building for weeks! And *Dieu*, he wasn't a monk!

Two weeks without sight of her in the flesh! Oh, he'd seen plenty in the press. Plenty enough to tease him and drive him half mad. Plenty of dated coy shots with the Prince too. And he wasn't a jealous man. He *wasn't*.

'Then why aren't you kissing me?'

'Because I don't believe in taking what I want without express permission.'

'I am granting you permission, Hugo. Right

here…' She pressed her body up against him, hooked her hands around his neck. 'Right now.'

And then she kissed him, and this time, he quit thinking. He quit every sense that wasn't all about her and took all that she was offering because consequences were tomorrow's concern.

Or today's, depending on how one looked at it.

Only he wasn't looking, he was living in the moment and loving every second.

Cassie was no virgin.

The Prince may have gone elsewhere for fun but he'd done his 'duty' by her. And that was just it. He'd always made it feel like a duty. Like it was all about producing an heir and never about desire. Never about lust. Fire. *This!*

And Cassie *was* on fire. Her entire body combusting with an explosive passion that she couldn't contain. She'd known her feelings for Hugo were growing out of her control but this…this raging heat in her bloodstream, this tension coiling through her body, this liquid heat pooling in her abdomen… She was kind of…scared.

'Hugo,' she panted, clawing at his chest through his T-shirt as she tore her mouth from his so that she could stare up at him, wide-eyed and dazed.

'Yes?'

'This is…'

'Crazy. Insane. Ill-advised.'

She gave a choked laugh. 'Yes!'

'You want me to stop, because I will.'

'No! Hell no.'

'Dieu Merci!'

She tugged him back to her kiss, marvelling at the way their mouths fit so perfectly together. The way his tongue teased and tangled with her own. Georges had never kissed her like this. With such passion, such intensity. Like he wanted all of her and more.

He walked her back into some hard surface, and she felt it rock. Heard something fragile rattle and he flicked a hand out to catch whatever it was without breaking tempo or the exploration of his kiss.

'Though we should take this to the bedroom before something hits the deck that shouldn't…'

She nodded and twisted in his arms, leading him down the corridor and into her room without pausing to turn on the lights. She was in too much of a hurry. Too scared that to pause would snuff out whatever this was building between them because *this* was what she had read about in books.

This was what she had seen on the TV.

This was what she had started to think was the stuff of make-believe…but was it possible that it was real after all?

Real and she could have it. With Hugo.

He spun her into his arms and she tore his T-shirt over his head before his mouth claimed hers once more. To be able to touch the body she had seen that first night, the broad shoulders, the chiselled pecs, the hard ridge of every ab…

She sighed into his mouth and he nipped her lip. 'Did you just sigh at me?'

'Maybe.'

'Sighing after sex is okay, but before?'

'I'm sorry, but your body is wholly satisfying.'

'I'll show you satisfying.'

And with that, he threw her back on the bed and stalked towards her.

'Wait!' She thrust out a hand and he paused, his cocked brow just visible in the light being cast from the outer hall.

'I'm all—' she wriggled against the sheets '—sweaty.'

'Believe me, you're going to be more

sweaty by the time I'm finished with you, *mon petit chaton.*'

She wanted to laugh. She wanted to cry. She wanted to thank the heavens for bringing her this man, because Georges would *never* have stood for 'sweaty her'. He'd have marched her to the shower, but Hugo, he was her *real* prince.

'In that case…' She relaxed, ran her teeth over her bottom lip as she thought of all that lay ahead. 'Come get me.'

Come get me? Have you heard yourself? And what about after, when he has your heart too? Because there can be no coming back from this!

The bed shifted with Hugo's weight and then he was beside her, his eyes level with hers, his hand in her hair and all her worries evaporated in the heat of his kiss.

Because everything felt right. So right and perfect.

Because Hugo made her *feel* just right and perfect just the way she was.

CHAPTER TEN

IF THE WEEKS prior to Hugo's leaving for New York had been incredible, the week following his return could be deemed nothing short of revelatory. And Cassie wasn't just referring to the orgasms, of which there had been many.

All to varying degrees of exemplariness.

Which was a word, right? Because it was Hugo all over when it came to being a lover. Attentive, thorough, going above and beyond.

Now she understood what a true climax was and there was only one problem with that discovery—it made them quite addictive. It made the *whole* act quite addictive.

And she was starting to feel like the harlot the Duponts would love to paint her as.

But it didn't count if you craved them all with the same man over and over, did it?

Though she digressed, because what she was really talking about was the *L* word itself and all the wondrous feelings that came with it.

There was no proving the opposite any more.

She was wholeheartedly and unequivocally in love with Hugo, and it was joyous.

She had gone her whole life without love, and finally she knew what it felt like to truly love another, and she was starting to hope that he felt the same. Because how could it be like this and not be reciprocated? How could *he* be like this and not feel it too?

'What's that grin about?'

He offered her a spoonful of Pierre's ice cream as he asked, the black and white movie they were watching playing over his features as they lay in her bed late one night...

It turned out Pierre's ice cream wasn't just perfect for a sunny Parisian autumnal day but the perfect post-make-out dish too.

'I was just thinking that you've turned me into a bit of a harlot.'

He chuckled. 'I think that technically a harlot has sex with multiple people for money, whereas you only do it with one man for Pierre's ice cream.'

'I was thinking that too.'

'So, you admit it, you do only have me for the ice cream?'

'Guilty as charged.'

'Why you…' In seconds he had the bowl shoved aside and he was upon her, tickling her ribs until she was laughing uncontrollably.

'Hugo, stop! Stop!'

'Not until you—'

And then he froze. Her body fenced in by his thighs as he rose above her, ears attuned to the outside world. 'Do you hear that?'

'What?'

And then she heard it. The rumble of people in the outer hall.

His phone started to ring and he sprang off the bed, reaching for it as he tugged on his lounge pants. Her mouth dry despite the recent ice cream, she eyed him, naked from the waist up. Would she ever be immune to him? She hoped not.

'Oui?' He blurted into his phone and his frown sharpened. *'Quoi?'*

His eyes launched to hers and she tensed—was he grey or was it the movie?

Please let it be the movie.

Are you okay? she mouthed, pushing herself to sitting.

The smallest shake of his head.

'Je viens.' He hung up the phone. 'I have to go.'

'Now?'

It was like *déjà vu.* Two weeks ago, the same thing had happened. The same wall had gone up. Work again? Or something else? But it was late, a Sunday too.

Though his companies were global, operating 24-7. She got that, but still.

'My parents are here.'

'Your *parents*?' She launched out of the bed, swept a hand over her wild hair. 'Oh, my God!'

'Exactly.'

She covered her mouth and stared at him. His parents. They were *here*? Across the hall? Right *now*? The parents of the man that she… that she *loved*. That was huge. A big deal. She swallowed.

She wanted to meet them. But not in her— not in her *underwear*. She'd dress first. But how did she broach that without broaching the real question of what they were. Him and her. For real. Not pretend. Because one couldn't meet the parents without first knowing how they would be introduced.

Because yes, they'd spent a week wrapped up in one another. To the outside world, nothing had changed, but behind closed doors *everything* had changed.

The problem was, neither of them had spoken of it. There'd been no heart-to-heart. Because she hadn't wanted to rock the boat. Too scared that she would push him away. Ruin whatever this was between them when it was too new, too fragile.

'Do they know about us?' she asked instead.

'I told my father we had an arrangement.'

'Oh.' Her heart gave a little shiver. That was news to her. And an arrangement wasn't a lie. It had been…in the beginning. 'When?'

He raked a hand over his hair, blew out a breath. 'A fortnight or so ago. The news got through to him so he called me, and I explained we were doing it for show.'

'You didn't say.'

'I didn't think I needed to. I wasn't expecting them to just turn up like this.'

'What are you going to tell them now?'

'Damned if I know, but I best go.'

She winced as her nails bit into her palms and he started for the door. 'Wait!'

He paused, angling his head just enough to eye her.

'Can I—? Do you want me to come too?'

'I don't think that's a good idea.'

'What about tomorrow?' She tried for a smile, though inside she could feel herself wilting. 'Perhaps we could take them for breakfast together somewhere?'

She could see the muscle working in his jaw—he didn't like the idea. Not one bit.

'Maybe. Let me just get the lay of the land first, yeah? See what's going on.'

She fought to keep her smile in place. 'Sure.'

He went to move off again.

'Hugo?'

He stopped.

'Aren't you forgetting something?'

She picked his T-shirt up off the floor, where she'd carelessly tossed it only an hour ago, when life had felt so very different, so very perfect. How was that possible? She wanted to bury her face in it and breathe in his scent. Relive that moment and the man he'd been then, to suppress the tears that wanted to fall now. Instead, she lifted her chin and handed it over.

'Thanks.'

And for a world-stilling moment she feared he would leave without a kiss goodbye. And when he bowed his head and swept his lips against her cheek for the briefest most heart-stealing kiss, she almost wished he had.

'*Bonne nuit*, Cassie.'

'Goodnight, Hugo.'

She gripped her middle, holding herself back when she wanted to race after him and confess all. Knowing that now wasn't the time. He needed to see his parents. He needed to deal with that challenge alone. Then they could face the next one together—their future and what it looked like.

Because she knew what she wanted.

The question was, did Hugo want it too?

'Maman. Papa. What are you doing here?'

'Hugo! Is that any way to greet your parents?' His mother hurried up to him, cheeks glowing from her time in the sun, but it was her eyes that truly sparkled. She looked joyous as they exchanged air kisses before she cupped his cheeks to take a closer look at his face. Her intense scrutiny heightened his nerves. 'How could you not tell me?'

'Tell you what?'

She smiled wide, patted his chest as she swirled away and took the drink his father now held out for her. In the time it had taken for Hugo to cross the hall and enter his home,

his father had been let in by his team and
made himself at home in the bar because, of
course, he had. *What's yours is mine and mine
is mine*, would be his father's motto forever.

'What's going on?'

'What do you think is going on, son? Your
mother has discovered the news and was too
excited to stay in paradise. She *had* to come
and see it for herself.' His father raised his
own glass in false cheer. 'Did you not want
to bring the Princess with you?'

If looks could kill...

'Don't look so cross with your father, Hugo.
It was my idea we turn up unannounced. I
wanted to surprise you.'

He dragged his gaze back to his mother.
'Surprise me, why?'

Now she looked sheepish. 'I know you had
us on that blissful retreat all these weeks, so I
understand that you may not have wanted to
break the rules to share your news, but something of this magnitude, darling. Don't you
think you could have at least let a note slip in,
given us just a little hint at your happiness.'

'My happiness?'

His eyes flitted to his father. Had he not
told his mother the truth? Was that a sparkle

in his father's eye, and to what end? Was he playing some kind of game with him?

'Father hasn't told you?'

'Told me what?'

'I figured this was your mess, son. You could be the one to explain it.'

'Mess? What do you mean? Will you two stop behaving like children and just explain.'

Hugo strode up to the bar and poured himself the same drink—like father like son. Only they weren't. They were chalk and cheese. And that was part of the problem. Why he was such a disappointment. Hugo wore his heart on his sleeve far too much for dear old dad. And he wasn't about to do it now.

'We're not in a relationship. Dad should have told you.'

Yet you were making love with her not an hour ago.

'I've been helping her out of a bad situation with her ex.'

And helping her into a new one with you.

'It's all an act for the cameras.'

An act that's been getting ever more real behind closed doors.

He threw back the drink with a wince.

'And you knew this and you didn't tell me, Antoni!' His mother rounded on his father.

'Don't blame me, Mary. I was on the retreat with you, remember.'

'But you knew all along!'

'I didn't know before he embarked on this whole debacle. If I had, I would have had something to say about it.'

His mother sank onto the edge of the sofa as she seemed to fizzle out before Hugo's eyes, and he scratched at his chest, the same sensation happening within him. And he felt his father's gaze on him, observing it all.

'Can you give us a second, Mary?'

His father's tone brooked no argument, and that's when Hugo knew, the real reason they were here was yet to come. His mother may think they were here because she wanted to be. Because she wanted to have it out with her son, the relationship she believed he'd been keeping a secret from her and to meet the woman she'd hoped had brought him happiness. But his father…

Slowly she got to her feet.

'The guest room is made up, Maman. You'll have all you need in there. I'll come and see you shortly.'

She looked so deflated, and he wanted to take it all back. The secret and the lies. He wanted to promise her the world with Cassie at the very top. Because hell, in a perfect world where he could have everything he wanted he would have that. Of course he would.

But a perfect world did not exist. Not for people like him. He'd believed in it once, and look where it had got him.

'We need to talk,' his father said as soon as his mother was out of earshot.

'Yeah, I got that.'

'It's about Sara.'

'I got that too.'

'I don't think you do, son.'

His knuckles flashed white around the glass, his eyes barely lifting from the drink as his father handed him his phone with a draft press article already active. There was the woman from his past, only she was very much in the present. She looked the same. Her warm caramel eyes, rich dark hair, alluring smile...

And there was his every flaw printed in black and white. Everything he had done wrong. His mistakes laid bare. The bodyguard who'd put his heart before his head and almost got her killed. Crossed a line when on duty. An absolute embarrassment. Brought shame on the company, on his family, and on hers.

'You need to bury this before it buries you and brings shame on her.'

He swallowed. Nodded.

And then he saw the profile shot of the reporter who had written the article. Frozen human snowman himself. How he must have loved getting his hands on this story. He shoved the phone back at his father. It didn't matter who had found the story, or how old a tale it was, it would be today's news tomorrow.

'Has Mum seen this?'

'Not yet. A friend gave me an advance read, but it'll be everywhere come tomorrow. Sara's family won't be happy.'

'It reads like it *came* from her family. A way to get their own back now that it won't affect them.'

'Perhaps.'

'I'll deal with it.'

'I'm sure you will. And what about the Princess?'

'Her name's Cassie.'

'Princess Cassandra. Cassie. They are one and the same.'

'They're really not.'

He could sense the curiosity in his father's gaze and avoided his eye. 'She goes by Cassie. And I'll talk to her.'

'I meant, what about this relationship you have going on? How long do you plan on keeping this up now this is soon to be out there? If it really is as fake as you say it is…'

He gripped the back of his neck with a curse. What a mess! What an absolute mess!

So tell him it's not. Tell him things are different now. That it's real. You can't, can you? Because the idea terrifies you.

He'd been so happy in their bubble of the past week.

Refusing to put a label on what they were now.

Refusing to think on what came next.

'She hardly needs this kind of a scandal following her about, Hugo.'

'Are you referring to me as some kind of an albatross around her neck, Father?'

'If the shoe fits. People like the Princess— *like* Cassie.' He changed it up with the look Hugo sent him, his brown eyes softening with what could even be interpreted as compassion. 'Like Sara, they come from another walk of life, son, and the sooner she goes back to it the sooner you can go back to yours. Before you get embroiled in her further… I've seen the way you look at her.'

'You haven't been here to see us together.'

'The photos are telling enough.'

'You don't know what you're—'

His father cut him off with the arch of a brow, and Hugo's chest tightened around the rest of his denial, the rest of his lie, because ultimately, his father was right. Cassie did come from another walk of life, just as Sara had. And she would return to that life and she would launch her career in fashion. She would forget about him and she wouldn't just survive, she would shine.

And if he thought life without Sara had hurt, life without Cassie…?

'Can we not do this now, please?'

'All those years I tried to make you more like me, harder, emotionally closed off,' his father said over him, 'but you had too much of your mother in you. When Sara came along, I knew she was trouble from day one. I saw what was happening and let it run its course, hoping it would teach you a lesson and I almost lost you in the process. This time I won't be so stupid. Don't be so foolish, son. Women like them, they're trouble. Why can't you find someone steady, someone home worthy, someone like—'

'Someone like me?'

'Mary!'

They both turned to find his mother stood in the hallway looking about ready to scream blue murder. 'So that is how you see me, Antoni?'

Oh, Dieu, here goes...

In a moment of madness, he thought about returning to Cassie. To escape the fight and find solace with her. But in mere hours the press would be pounding the streets outside, and his age-old wound would be tomorrow's tittle-tattle.

How did he even begin to bury it?

He didn't know, but he had to try.

Cassie barely slept a wink.

Funny how one could sleep alone for months, but a week with another and your body suddenly depended on that person to be there.

When her phone rang at the crack of dawn, she was grateful for the interruption. Grateful all the more to hear Louis's excited chatter on the other end offering to pay her for the designs she had finally sent over. A collaboration to get the name Cassie Couture out into the world—yes, please.

It was what she needed. What she'd wanted for so long. Only it landed…flat.

'You are happy—*oui*?'

'*Oui*, Louis. *Oui.*'

'You do not sound it? What is wrong, Cassie? I can…maybe offer you some more money. Is it not enough? Let me see. What about—'

'No, Louis. It's fine. Honest. More than fine. I promise.'

'Then what is it? Is it that Hugo? I bet it is! He is a big man. A beast! I am coming home tomorrow. I will sort him out!'

She gave a hitched laugh. 'No—No, Hugo is fine. We are fine.'

'I don't believe you. Don't lie to me.'

'Louis, behave. All is good. I will see you tomorrow.'

'*Oui, bien.* And then I will see you for myself and we will celebrate. Champagne! *Ciao*, darling.'

'*Ciao.*'

She hung up, a sad smile on her lips. She didn't even have the energy for a morning run. Instead, she got dressed and took her coffee out onto the balcony, watched the sun rise and Paris wake up. Surprised when the doorbell rang not long after.

Her heart did a little jig. It was too early for Housekeeping and her heart did what it always did now—it sprang to Hugo.

She peered through the peephole to find an

older woman on the other side. Dark hair to her shoulders, same heart-shaped brow, same blue eyes—Hugo's mother!

She eased open the door, trying to second-guess if this was a good sign or a bad sign. Could Hugo have sent her? And if he had, that would most definitely be good, wouldn't it?

'*Bonjour*, I hope you don't mind me calling by.' Her French accent was thick, her eyes and smile both warm and welcoming. 'But since my son was so rude as to keep you a secret for over a month, I thought I would introduce myself. I'm Hugo's mother.' She held out her hand, which Cassie took, and she gently covered Cassie's with her other. 'Mary Chevalier.'

'It's a pleasure to meet you, Mrs Chevalier. I'm Cassie.'

'So I hear.' Her smile widened as she released her. 'And you can call me Mary. Can I tempt you to breakfast, Cassie?'

'Erm…sure.' She stepped back. 'Would you like to come in?'

'I thought we might go out.'

'Out?' Cassie gulped. 'Just me and you?'

'*Oui.*'

'Does Hugo know?' She looked across the hall at his very closed door and Mary nipped her lip, leaning in conspiratorially.

'I won't tell if you won't.'

Cassie gave a nervous laugh. She couldn't help it. Now she understood where Hugo got his playful spirit from.

And what could it hurt, really? Though what did his mother know, exactly? Had Hugo told her the truth about them…were they fake…were they real…?

The problem was, not even Cassie knew the answer to that. Not from the all-important man himself.

But this was a chance to get to know more about Hugo. Hugo from before she knew him. Hugo from his mum's perspective. And if she knew more, maybe she could find a way to make this into more for him too.

'Let me get my purse…'

Hugo woke to laughter.

The kind of laughter that had no place in his penthouse. Two women. His mother and— *Cassie?*

He shot out of bed, following the ruckus into the kitchen, and there they were. The two thick as thieves, wearing aprons and smiles and an abundance of good cheer.

'What in the love of—?'

'Ah, Hugo!' His mother swept towards him

and clamped her flour-covered hands on his cheeks as she kissed him. '*Bonjour!* Cassie and I are making your favourite!'

'My *what*?'

'Madeleines, of course!'

'Madeleines?' he repeated.

'Yes, French madeleines.' His father put down the newspaper he was reading at the table before the window and eyed him over his glasses. 'It's good of you to join us.'

Hugo ran his hands over his hair. Had he walked into some strange parallel universe, because this could not be his life today?

And then he heard it, the frenzy outside. The press. It was like the day after the night before. Or rather, the day after the flower photo had broken. Only now it wasn't him with flowers on her doorstep that had sparked the uprising, it was his decade-old failing. Almost getting a woman killed. So much for spending half the night awake, calling in favours and doing what he could to smother it.

But this laughter, this chaos in his kitchen, it was all about distracting him from it. Pretending it wasn't happening. It had to be.

And Cassie was here. Smothering herself in his shame when she should be distancing herself, getting as far away from him as she could.

He shook his head. The pounding within not thanking him for the gesture.

'Maman. Papa. Can you give us a moment, *please*?'

'I think it better you give *us* a moment, because we don't want to let the little madeleines burn.' His mother gave him a wink. A wink!

And he reached for Cassie's hand, pulling her from the room without looking at her because if he looked at her, all cute and homely in her apron, with flour on her cheeks, in her hair—*gah!*

He was going to surrender on the spot.

Too much emotion trying to overrun his good sense, and then where would he be?

Out of control of his life and lost to it. Just like he'd been all those years ago. His life in pieces with no way of knowing how to pull it back together again.

'You shouldn't be here.' He closed his bedroom door and stalked to the window, looked down over the Champs-Élysées and the hovering journalists demanding their ounce of blood, *his* blood this time, and yanked the shutters closed.

'Why?'

'You must have seen the reports?'

'You mean the stuff about Sara?'

She said it like it was nothing. How could she say it like it was *nothing*? 'Yes!'

She walked towards him and he backed away. 'It's okay, Hugo. It'll all blow over soon enough. It'll be yesterday's news. They'll print something else and the world will forget and—'

'But *I* won't. I won't forget what I did.' He pounded his chest with his fist, spat the words out. '*I* won't forget how it felt.'

She covered his palm with her hand, and he flinched away as though burnt. 'Don't. Don't touch me.'

'But Hugo, you—'

'*Please*, Cassie!' Because she was killing him. *It* was killing him. This feeling. Crushing him inside. Suffocating him. The same feeling as back then, only it cut so much deeper now. 'You need to stay away from me. You deserve someone who won't bring this to your door. *You* deserve more. *You* deserve better.'

'Don't do that. Don't stick me on some pedestal like my parents did, telling me who I should or shouldn't be seen with. Who is considered good enough for me. *I* choose those things. And I choose you.'

He shook his head so viciously he thought

he might be sick. Or was that just the rolling in his gut.

'I don't care what the press says any more, Hugo. I don't care what the world says. The only person I care about is you.'

He pressed his palms to his temples, pushing out her words. Because she couldn't mean them. She only thought she did because she had spent her whole life being treated so badly. So starved of love and affection that to have known it through him these past few weeks, she now felt him worthy of it in return. But he *wasn't* worthy of it. And she would see that once she got out in the world and experienced it properly. Once he freed her of the hold he had inadvertently cast over her.

'I can't do this any longer, Cassie.'

'Do what?'

He threw a hand towards the kitchen— at the baking and his mother's presence, all mixed up in Cassie's. All homely and sweet and nice. 'Live this lie.'

'Which lie? The fake relationship to the press or the real one we have…'

He shook his head, trying to cut her off, and she gave a shaky laugh and wrapped her arms around her middle.

'Because I know you told your parents it

was fake too. But your mother took me for breakfast this morning, and she made it pretty clear that she thinks it's quite real and—'

'No, Cassie!'

Hugo stared back at her, the tortured look in his blue eyes crushing her with his words.

'No, Cassie?' she repeated softly. 'What do you mean, "no"?'

Though she knew, could already feel the chasm so vast between them.

'So, it's over,' she said, when he failed to speak. 'Whatever this was, it's over. You and me. This?'

Still nothing. Barely a flicker of his dark lashes over eyes that still raged a storm.

'Fine.' She lifted her chin, stood tall as if she owned her feelings and wanted him to know them too. That way there could be no confusion between fact and fiction when she was gone. 'But since we're done with the lies, Hugo, here's my truth—I love you.'

He blanched, and she wanted to choke on her own heart.

'Yes, I know you don't want to hear it, but tough. I do. You have given me so much. You have shown me how to live and to love and for that I will always be grateful to you.'

He'd gone so very pale, his eyes so very vacant. She pleaded with him to say something, anything, but…nothing.

'As for going forward, I'm moving out. Louis is coming back tomorrow, so you won't need to see me every day either. You can count your blessings there too.'

Still, nothing.

'Goodbye, Hugo.'

And she walked before her legs refused to function and she crumbled at his feet. Because she refused to let him see how broken she truly was.

She would be okay. She had her future. She had Cassie Couture. She had her whole life ahead of her. Her dreams were coming true.

Even if Hugo wasn't to be a part of them any more, it was better to have loved and lost than never to have loved at all.

And she truly believed that, having known it now, pain and all.

CHAPTER ELEVEN

Three days later

'IF YOU HADN'T made him feel so worthless growing up, maybe he'd feel worthy of her now.'

'And if you hadn't made him feel so soft, maybe he would have been man enough to fight for her.'

Hugo gawped at his parents, who had made themselves right at home on his sofa.

'Will you two just stop, please. This isn't helping.'

'Well, if you'd been honest with me about how you felt, son.'

'You didn't give him the chance to be honest, Antoni. You were too busy throwing Sara back at him!'

'*I* messed this up, Maman. Me! Nobody else!'

Now his parents gawped at *him* and he dropped his gaze to the note in his hand, fighting the reflex that would have seen it crumpled and creased. Scarcely able to believe the words on the card that had accompanied the bouquet of classic cream hydrangeas now on his coffee table.

He would think it some twisted joke of the paparazzi if he didn't know Cassie's elegant scrawl as well as his own handwriting, having pored over enough of her detailed fashion designs…

> *My darling Hugo,*
> *I am sorry for what has come to pass.*
> *It was never my intention to hurt you, nor to fall in love with you.*
> *The press are my cross to bear, and what was printed in your name will pain me for ever. Because, as Wellington once said of Napoleon, you are worth forty thousand men—to my mind, you are worth all the men in the world. Because I have never met one such as you.*
> *My heart is yours.*
> *Always and for ever.*
> *Cassie xxx*

He strode up to the window, stared out over the streets of Paris, wondering which one was lucky enough to offer up a home to her now. Because to write the note by hand at the local florist he'd used himself all those weeks ago, meant she had to be in the city somewhere… only where?

He wanted to throw open the French windows and call her name from the rooftops, beg her to come home.

'This was my mistake and now I need to fix it,' he said, his breath misting up the chilled pane of glass. But how did he fix it when he didn't know where she was?

Louis was refusing to speak to him, so there wasn't a chance in hell he'd give away her location.

He pressed his fist against the window, gritted his teeth. How could he have been so stupid as to let her walk away? The one woman he had come to love with his all. The one woman who had chosen to love him with her all, and he had thrown it back in her face. Rejected it. All because he had deemed himself unworthy of it. How stupid could he be?

What he would give to be able to rewind to that night or that morning, he didn't care which, and make it right. Tell her the truth. Tell her that he loved her. That he'd always love her and only her.

'You know she has Lyon's security working for her.'

Hugo's ears pricked at his father's less than subtle comment. 'Lyon?'

'*Tak.* She asked me if I could recommend a close protection firm…after giving me what for.'

He turned his head. 'She gave you what for?'

'A bit like your mother's doing now. Some nonsense about not telling you I was proud of you enough. That if I'd loved you a bit more, then maybe you'd have accepted her love rather than thrown it back in her face.'

He huffed and his mother gasped. 'You didn't tell me that, Antoni.'

'Yes, well, it was hardly my finest moment to share.' His father cleared his throat and squeezed his mother's hand before getting to his feet and crossing the room. 'And it wasn't nonsense at all. She was right. And I'm sorry for that, son. Because I wish it wasn't the case. You're not me, and neither should I have tried to make you so. You always used this first.'

He touched his hand to Hugo's chest. The contact as surprising as the compassion in his father's brown gaze. So he hadn't imagined its presence the other day either but…his father, compassionate?

'Are you—are you *crying*, Father?'

'No. Absolutely not.'

'You could have fooled me.'

'But I am concerned about Cassie's well-being.'

'Why?' he blurted, all teasing forgotten as worry for her overtook all else. 'Why would you say that?'

'Because she's taken to running along the river at some ungodly hour in the morning like she's got some kind of death wish.'

Hugo's mouth quirked.

'I can't imagine why anyone in their right mind would do such a thing, but she's out there with a team every night like clockwork. Lyon is quite amused by it all and I told him in no uncertain terms he should quit laughing and talk some sense into her.'

'We used to go together.'

'You are joking.'

'No!' He grasped his father by his arms and planted a smacker on his cheek. 'Thank you, Papa!'

'What for?' he chortled.

'For giving me an idea.'

'You're not going to accost her at that time of night on the Seine? Surely?'

'It's our thing.'

His father eyed him dubiously. 'That's some *thing.*'

It really was, and it was all he needed… he hoped.

The witching hour wasn't the same without Hugo. It didn't stop Cassie trying to find its magic though. The peace, the rush, the joyous feeling between night and day when she could run and let go…or at least try and let go of the stress that plagued her through the day and wouldn't let her sleep at night.

That is, thoughts of Hugo and her love for him and the conversation that she knew could have gone better if she'd perhaps given him a little more time to adjust to his parents' homecoming. Hadn't ambushed him with his mother. Hadn't dumped the *L* word on him.

She toyed with going back. Every night she ran a loop that took her past the Avenue des Champs-Élysées and every night she chickened out. Failing to find her peace, the rush, the magic, and her Hugo, all at the same time.

Because of course he didn't love her. How could he? She'd spent her life trying to earn the love of her parents, then the Prince. Why would Hugo be any different?

Because he is different, came the honest answer.

He was kind. He was good. He was honourable.

And she was glad she had met him, even if she had lost her heart to him and feared she would never feel quite whole again.

And she was glad she had sent him an apology too, because he hadn't deserved all that bad press over an isolated incident that had happened so long ago. Maybe if she'd read the articles, given them the time of day, she might have understood why they had cut so deep. But she hadn't wanted to. She hadn't wanted to justify a single word they had printed by dedicating a single second of screen time to them.

But she'd made herself read them in the aftermath. Having witnessed his torment, his self-loathing, his pain. She'd made herself read every word and had hated the journalist as much as she had hated herself for provoking him enough to go to the lengths it must have taken to uncover such a story. And she had hated the world for making it okay to print such words about the man she loved. Words that had cut open a wound that had barely healed, forcing her to leave him bleeding and in pain.

His reputation torn to shreds. His masculinity. His pride. His father's disappointment. His love lost. Not to mention the news spreading within his security company. How it must feel to know that he would have rookies reading the article, learning of his mistakes… All thanks to her.

'Ma'am, you need to slow down. There's someone up ahead.'

Jody, one of her close protection detail, came up alongside her and nodded to a guy as he rounded the exit of the Pont Neuf bridge. Cassie's heart fluttered in her chest. Recognising his broad frame before her eyes did.

'*Hugo?*'

'Ma'am?'

'It's Hugo!'

And she wasn't slowing down, she was speeding up. Racing towards him, because she knew, knew with every beat of her pulse that it was Hugo. Her Hugo. And there could be only one reason he would be here at this time of night…

'Ma'am!' Jody hurried after her, but Cassie was sprinting and so was Hugo.

'Cassie!'

'It's okay, Jody! It's Hugo! I know him! I know him!'

They came together in a collision of bodies, the air forced from her lungs as his arms closed around her and he hugged her to his chest. 'Cassie!'

He breathed her name into her hair, his voice as pained as the grip around her.

'What are you doing here, Hugo?'

'I had to see you.'

She prised herself back enough to look up at his face, his eyes glittering in the lamplight. Lines of worry creased up his brow, bracketed his mouth—the man had aged a decade in a week and still looked like the sexiest man to walk the earth.

'Is everything okay?'

'*No*. Nothing is okay.'

'Let me guess, you're not sleeping very well again?'

'Hardly a wink.'

'So you've come to hijack my witching hour?'

'If you'll let me.'

'Is this to escape your parents?'

He choked on a laugh, his big strong hands lifting to cup her face as his eyes searched hers in wonder. 'No. For once it is not my parents. Though I'm having a tough time getting rid of them.'

'Then…'

'It is you, Cassie.' He took a ragged breath that vibrated through her too as he kept her ever close. 'It's this pain I now have inside of me because I was fool enough to let you walk away.'

'Then why did you? Why hurt us both so much?'

'Because I refused to accept your love. That for all you said you loved me, I refused to accept I could be worthy of it. But the truth is, I am too selfish to let you go, which probably means I'm even more unworthy of it.'

He gave another choked laugh, his fingers trembling against her face.

'What are you saying, Hugo?'

He lifted the rim of her cap to ease it off her head and the cool night air teased along her skin.

'I'm saying many things. I'm saying I let my fear of getting hurt a second time around get in the way of us. I'm saying I refused to accept the truth of what was there all along. I'm saying my mother was right. I'm saying you were right. I'm saying this is real, Cassie.

I am saying that I love you. With all my heart, I love you.'

She blinked up at him, her heart racing a million miles a second. 'You do?'

'I think I loved you the moment you came to my naked rescue. Loved you all the more when you stuck that ice cream cone on that jerk's nose. And I will continue loving you all the more if you can forgive me for being too foolish to accept it and hurting you in the process. I can't *bear* that I hurt you.'

'Oh, Hugo!' Tears filled her eyes, her throat, and she launched herself up, kissed him with all the love she felt inside. 'I'm sorry too. So very sorry. I never meant to hurt you. I never meant for all that stuff with Sara to get dredged up. I never—'

He kissed her deep, unrelenting, fierce. Lifting her off the ground as he pressed her body to his. 'You don't need to apologise,' he growled against her lips. 'That wasn't you. That was them. And I choose to no longer care too. My past is my past. It's a part of me and I can't change that.'

'And I'm not so sure you should… I kind of like the man you are.'

'You "kind of *like*" or do you still…?' He cocked one sexy brow and she chuckled.

'Oh, Hugo, are you fishing?'

'It's three in the morning, Cassie, give a man a break?'

She ducked his arms and backed into the middle of the bridge, her arms and smile wide as she twirled on the spot, glossy ponytail swinging out. *'Écoute, Paris! J'aime Hugo Chevalier de tout mon cœur!'*

He chucked as she steadied herself to say, 'Was that loud enough for you?'

'You're going to get us arrested.' He chuckled as he walked up to her.

'Well, I mean it, Hugo. I love you with all of my heart.'

'And I love you, *mon petit chaton.*'

And then he tugged her to him and kissed her, and Cassie knew that this was it.

This was her love story. This was her man. It had taken thirty-three years and a wrong turn, but love and all its wondrous feelings was real. And it was worth waiting for.

EPILOGUE

September, two years later,
Paris Fashion Week

ROUNDING OFF FASHION'S 'Big Four', with the final week in Paris, was a dream come true for Cassie. Her label was out there amongst the world's biggest names in global fashion, and hearing the ripple of adulation and applause from the audience made up of fashion editors, writers, buyers, stylists, influencers, celebrities—*all* the people she needed to impress—was as joyous as exiting the Louvre on the arm of the man she loved. Her husband.

And she wasn't just exiting on the red carpet, she was walking on air because she had a piece of news to share with the man who had helped to make those dreams come true.

'Cassie! Hugo! Can we get a smile?'

He paused beside her, looking so very sexy in black tie. 'What do you say?'

She pulled her shimmering silver train to one side so that she could turn and smile up at him, remembering a time many moons ago. 'Do I have food on my face?'

He returned her smile, his eyes as wistful as hers as he cupped her cheek and swiped his thumb along her lower lip. All the love in the world shining in his gaze and she couldn't wait to tell him. Was surprised he couldn't read her confession in her gaze.

'Do you think they'll get bored of that move?'

'Never. I told you, as much as they love to play the viper, they're just a bunch of old romantics who love a good love story.'

'Love story,' she said with him.

'Exactly.'

She kissed his thumb. 'I love you.'

'I love you too.'

The cameras went crazy—flashes going off, reporters cooing. Not that she was paying any attention to them—she was all about her man and the love overflowing within her.

'Shall we go home?'

'I thought you'd never ask.'

She led him to their awaiting car, pausing just long enough to say goodbye to all those that needed to be thanked. Good wishes exchanged. Promises to call. Meetings to be arranged passed to her very attentive PA.

He chuckled as soon as they were strapped into the rear seat of their limo, the privacy glass between them and the driver giving them the quiet they so desperately desired. 'Thought we'd never be free.'

She scooted into his side. 'But we're worth the wait, right?'

'We're always worth the wait, *mon petit chaton.*'

She smiled. 'When I said "we" I wasn't referring to you and me… I was referring to—' she took his hand and pressed it against her tummy '—all of us. Another, even littler kitten.'

He tensed and his breath caught. 'Cassie! You're not. We're not.'

She nodded and peeped up at him. 'We're pregnant. I found out this morning, but with everything happening and we hadn't a moment to—'

He stole her explanation with his kiss, his elation in every impassioned sweep of his mouth against hers. When finally, he came up for air, his crystal-blue eyes glistened down at her.

'I never thought I could be happier than the

day you told me you loved me. You've just proved me wrong.'

'In that case, our child proved us both wrong, because I feel the exact same way.'

'Just wait until my mother finds out.'

'Your mother? It's your father who keeps nagging about grandchildren.'

He gave a soft huff as he swept her hair back from her face and searched her gaze, his own filled with wonder. 'I can't believe he is the same man. Retirement has been the making of him.'

'Or maybe it's just softened him, giving him the chance to indulge that side of him that was always there.'

'And for that I'm glad.'

'Me too. You have a good relationship.'

'We do now. As do you.'

Her smile quivered about her lips. 'Thank heaven. I'm blessed to have that with both of your parents.'

'They feel lucky to have you too. A daughter they're very proud of.'

He'd guessed where her head was at. Thinking of what she didn't have with her own blood, but she'd come to terms with that long ago, and she wasn't going to shed any more tears over them. She'd reached out once, with news of her engagement to Hugo, and they'd made their 'disappointment' clear. She wasn't a punchbag, willing to go back for more.

If they wanted to change their attitude and come to her, they knew where to find her. And they could bring their apology with them.

But she wouldn't hold her breath.

She didn't need them. She was happy with the people whose happiness truly mattered to her. With those she loved and who loved her in return. Who valued her happiness as she did theirs. Her family. Hugo, his parents, and their little baby Chevalier.

* * * * *

*If you enjoyed this story,
check out these other great reads
from Rachael Stewart*

Unexpected Family for the Rebel Tycoon
Reluctant Bride's Baby Bombshell
My Unexpected Christmas Wedding
Off-Limits Fling with the Heiress

All available now!